MAJERA

Book 4 of the Kitra Saga

Gideon Marcus

Journey Press
journeypress.com

Vista, California
Journey Press

Journey Press
P.O. Box 1932
Vista, CA 92085
© Gideon Marcus, 2026

CREDITS
Interior art: © Lorelei Esther, 2026
Cover design: DLR Cover Designs, Jessica Holmes

First Printing February 2026

ISBN: 978-1-951320-33-1

Published in the United States of America

journeypress.com

To Juan, the original Fareedh.

Chapter One

Jub-Jub was trying to escape again.

I watched the half-meter long crustacean press against the edges of its enclosure. Gray claws and antennae trailed along the corners of the long and transparent box Marta had made for it, less the blind probing of a big bug and more like the purposeful exploration of a cat faced with a kitchen drawer it wants to play in.

Eventually, I put down my steaming mug of coffee, got up, and walked around the long table of Majera's wardroom, to work the release on the creature's clear terrarium. I scooped Jub-Jub into my arms, and it immediately settled down, flopping against me completely relaxed. I ran my short-nailed fingers over its hide–half leather, half chitin–and it snuggled even more. I'd long since stopped worrying about its talons or the vise-like mouth in its broad, stumpy head. Jub-Jub was a friendly soul, and anyway, nothing about me was tasty to it. My DNA spiraled the wrong way, or something like that, Marta had said. We'd had to program the Maker special to produce food Jub-Jub could eat.

Had we been cruel to take the little creature from its home? Jub-Jub's hadn't been a bad planet. You could breathe the air, sort of. And for Jub-Jub, it had been paradise, with more of its kind to play with and plenty of pools and marshes to frolic around in, making that peculiar sloshing sound that had inspired its name. Our little ship was nothing like Jub-Jub's homeworld, at least, his swampy corner of it. Even the light was different. Majera's ceiling panels glowed vaguely orange, like the sun back home on Vatan — six weeks away and across the starless Rift. Jub-Jub's sun had been yellow, part of the binary listed just as GM +156. The unromantic name made sense; no one had ever been this far out.

Marta had done her best to make Jub-Jub feel at home, and Lord knows the long, transparent box took up enough of Majera's wardroom, but it wasn't enough. Whenever I came in, to eat or make coffee or just to leave the confinement of my stateroom, the little thing started to click its claws and scrape against the clear wall of its enclosure. We'd only had it a week, and it already knew how to play on my heart strings.

And that's why I was holding an alien lobster when Pinky walked in.

"Looks like he's becoming quite attached to you," Pinky's baritone sang out. I turned to see my oldest and best friend pad his way out of his room, on three legs for the moment. His shapeless head stretched on an expanding neck so his two swirly eyespots could get a better view.

I tried to push Jub-Jub away, even a centimeter, but it dug its claws in tight. Pinky was right.

"I think it's just cold blooded," I said, giving up.

"Nonsense. You're irresistible." With that, he teetered, as if off balance, and made a show of collapsing onto me. I couldn't easily dodge, pinned between table and shelf, and with five kilos of alien crab clinging to me. Now Pinky's rubbery arms stretched around me, and I was well and truly trapped.

His eyespots rolled up. "See?"

"Great. I'm the gravitational center of the universe."

"Everything is at some point," he said. "It might as well be your turn."

For a moment, I had visions of Marta, Peter and Fareedh bounding from their rooms and adding to the snowball. It wasn't such a bad thought, provided they didn't come *too* quickly.

"What are you doing up so early?" I asked, absently petting Pinky's head with my free hand.

"Oh, I was going to see if Fareedh was up. I had a question about his character."

I smiled. He was still obsessing on that S&S campaign he'd started back on Hyvilma three weeks ago.

"At this hour? I'm the earliest bird, and it's early for *me*," I said.

"I just had a neat idea," he said cryptically. As usual, Pinky's featureless face betrayed nothing, but his rose coloration deepened slightly.

"Why don't you just comm him?" I asked.

He disengaged from his hug to free his arms for a shrug. "Where's the fun in that? Communication should be in person."

I chuckled. "Well, write it down or something so you don't forget."

Pinky radiated salmon with amusement, "When have I ever forgotten anything?"

"Fair point," I conceded, followed by "Ouch!" Jub-Jub had taken that moment to dig its claws into my shoulder. "All right, fella. Back home you go." It was reluctant, wrapping a pincer around my ponytail to keep from falling back inside the enclosure, but persistence and the ship's artificial gravity eventually won out, and the creature skittered back inside its little swamp. I quickly closed the terrarium.

"I have to wonder what Sirena would have made of that little guy," I said.

"*Ceviche*", Pinky said blandly.

I barked out a little laugh, then found my gaze flickering to the jamb of the door to the bridge where her highness Sirena Isabella de la Atlántida Jáimez, the Seventh, princess of Atlántida, had affixed her last motivational slogan before her departure. "*A ver a un velorio y a divertirse a un fandango*," which, when roughly translated into our native French, meant, 'Be serious when appropriate, but have fun when you can.'

The princess couldn't be having much fun right now. We'd left her on Hyvilma to help pick up the pieces after an abortive rebellion had swept the purple world, extending to the very decks of the imperial cruiser stationed in orbit to keep the peace. It was hardly what she'd signed up for when she'd contracted the *Majera* back on Vatan, so many weeks ago. A simple survey jaunt beyond the Rift had turned into a mission of mercy: 10,000 sleeping colonists had been stranded in the wrecked Émilie du Châtelet above their destination world, deep in the trans-Rift frontier, when their Drive vanished upon egress into normal space. We'd had to rescue them and help set up their new home on the planet, which the grateful emigres had named after Sirena.

As if that weren't excitement enough, on the way back to Hyvilma to register the colony, *Majera* had been ambushed by pirates and Pinky had gotten hurt fixing the ship. When we got to Hyvilma, the world had gotten embroiled in a civil war, with the cruiser *Faucon* the main battleground. I still couldn't believe how much we'd gotten entangled in that fight. The captain of the *Faucon* had called us heroes.

I'm no hero. I'd just needed everyone to stop shooting long enough to save my friend. The *Faucon* had the only hospital we could get to

Now, with the dust barely settled, Sirena was the neutral vote on the three-being commission trying to resolve the aftermath of the rebellion. There was no doubt Sirena was the right person for the job, with her diplomatic experience and maturity. It was the kind of role my mother would have taken, were she still alive. I just wished it hadn't taken Sirena away from *us*.

"What are you thinking about?" Pinky asked gently. I realized I must have been musing for a while.

"I don't think I ever really made the connection between Sirena and mom. Sirena's so flamboyant and unusual. But I guess they have a lot in common, now that I think about it," I said.

Pinky pulsed almost imperceptibly in agreement. "Your mother was a strong woman. I wish I'd had a chance to know her directly."

"She'd have loved you," I said and knew it was true. The secret to mom's success as an ambassador had been her capacity to love anyone, no matter their viewpoint. I ran my fingers over Pinky's head again, and he flushed a deep rose. After a moment, I asked, "How are you feeling? No more double-vision?"

"I never thought of looking at the world that way before. Hmm." Pinky's eye spots spread wide, and he made a show of wobbling a bit. "How interesting." His color slipped back to warm pink as his swirly dots focused to look up at me. "I'm all right. Still me. Thanks for asking."

I relaxed. Ever since he'd…merged, or exchanged, or whatever it was with Lieutenant L' éclair, communications officer on the *Faucon* and the one member of Pinky's race within twenty light years, he'd been a little different. It had been necessary to save Pinky's life, kind of a transfusion, I guess, but the encounter had changed them both. Pinky now had some of L' éclair's Navy secrets, and a couple of his quirks, notably in food preference. It had taken Pinky a while to sort out which parts of his personality were his and which were the other being's. As for the sober L' éclair, he might *never* recover. I'd heard from Fareedh's brother, now First Lieutenant on the *Faucon*, that L' éclair had inherited some of Pinky's unique sense of humor, which his crew might or might not appreciate.

The whir of a door receding into its wall jamb followed by a full-throated yawn caught my ears. I turned to see Fareedh saunter into the room dressed in a rainbow-striped nightshirt more blinding than hyperspace. Close behind was Peter, almost twice Fareedh's width, his pale features looking considerably more alert.

"Hey, you two," I said around a smile. "Late night?" Knowing them, they'd probably been fiddling with their *sayar* calculations or running simulations till the wee hours. I couldn't blame them — if I'd invented a way to Jump three parsecs without using any fuel, I'd spend all my time validating it, too.

Peter grinned sheepishly. "Does it show?"

"Not really," I said.

"After all," Pinky added helpfully, "your hair always looks like that."

I stifled a laugh. Peter's white-blonde hair was bristled like a rooster's crest. He self-consciously ran a smoothing hand through it.

Fareedh poured himself a mug from the coffee pot. He closed his eyes in appreciation as he breathed its vapor before taking a sip. The corners of his lips quirked upward. "I can always tell when Kitra makes the brew," he murmured.

"Too hot?" I asked.

He shook his head, his roughly bound ponytail of black hair wiggling on narrow shoulders. "I mean it's clear you didn't have the Maker print it. This is the real stuff."

I felt a glow of satisfaction. "Well, we Jump out tomorrow. I figured we'd live a little this morning."

His dark eyes flashed briefly. "You know how to live," he said, raising his mug in salute.

I smiled, then eagerly turned to Peter. "So what's our fuel at now?" I asked.

Peter rolled his eyes. "You ask that every morning. You could always check yourself."

"Where's the fun in that? Anyway, don't you have it on the tip of your tongue? Isn't that what you guys were doing all night?"

Fareedh shrugged. "All work and no play…"

"We processed the calcs from this latest Jump the first day after entering hyperspace," Peter broke in, programming his breakfast at the Maker station in the room's corner. "Even I'm satisfied the theory's sound. We spent the night playing *Starsea*."

"Among other things," Fareedh added idly, taking a seat at the table and blowing steam off of his mug.

Peter's back was to me, but I thought the tips of his ears might have flushed slightly. His expression was neutral, however, when he faced me, carrying a tray laden with oval cakes, butter melting on top. He set down the tray and spun his chair around, leaning heavily against the seat back.

"I'll recheck the calcs before Jump-out, promise," he said. "But since you asked, fuel use is nominal for in-Jump. We won't really know the effect on our hydrogen reserves until we slide out of Jump tomorrow, but this is the third test, and at this point, I'm willing to bet we don't use more than a percent on egress." He hooked a thumb at the terrarium. "I think we spend more juice heating Jub-Jub than we do on Jump."

I nodded. It still boggled me to think about it. For seven centuries, hurling a ship through hyperspace had taken a tremendous amount of fuel. The only improvement during that time was the distance one could hop. *Majera* was an old ship, built as a Navy scout almost a century ago. Fully fueled, it could Jump ten light years, if you weren't worried about your tanks being bone dry at the end of the trip.

At least, that's how it used to be, until Peter, using what he'd learned from the vanished Drive of the Émilie, had Jumped *Majera* at the edge of a planet's gravity well to escape from the pirates at GM +115, and we found ourselves, as Peter explained it, skating on hyperspace rather than plunging into it. I didn't pretend to understand. I know normal space, not the weird brain-searing expanse of the fifth dimension, or wherever it is *Majera* goes on its one-week trips between stars.

Now, the only fuel we burned in the ship's plant was what we used firing engines or running the gravity thrusters in normal space. Our interstellar range was still the same, or at least, we hadn't tried to test going beyond it. Not yet. But the fuel used to go in and out of Jump, normally the biggest expenditure, was now essentially zero. We'd spent the last three Jumps proving that it could be done consistently. It was something that was going to change humanity forever, as much as the balloon flight of the Montgolfier brothers or Ansari's trip to Alpha Centauri.

I should have been thrilled. For reasons I hadn't quite parsed, I wasn't. I went to make my own breakfast. I didn't want to snow on their dance.

"So what's the plan for today after we eat?" I asked over my shoulder.

Pinky cocked his eyespots slantwise. "You have to ask? Your party is still stuck in that asteroid belt, you know."

I snorted a little laugh. Of course. Well, there were worse ways to spend time in hyperspace than marathon sessions of Spaceships and Supernovas...

That night, I lit the Sabbath candles.

It had been a long time, so long that I almost felt guilty. I faltered as I started to sing the blessing, but reflexes kicked in, and my voice strengthened. The two candles flickered, casting dancing shadows on their small table and against the walls of my dimly lit cabin, glinting off the treasures of my Exhibit Table.

When I was young, the Sabbath had been an exciting time. On mom's embassy ship, it seemed to come so arbitrarily. All of a sudden *this* day we would stop our work, light the candles, say the prayers, make a feast. And, of course, we split into two groups at prayers, with two different books. Half of the crew would then take the next 24 shipboard hours off while the other half took their shifts that day with no compunctions.

Over centuries of starfaring, the Jewish faith of my mother had so merged with the faith of my Muslim father's ancestors that they had become almost intertwined, two sides of the same coin. I don't think I was even aware of a distinction between Judaism and Islam until after mom had died. In any event, dad had been gone long before that, so whatever he might have taught me was mostly lost in my early youth. It wasn't until Fareedh had invited me to one of his family's prayer nights that I really grasped the subtle differences.

Fareedh wasn't a great gateway to my father's world, though; his faith had lapsed almost to nonexistence. Dozens of weeks had gone by since we'd started traveling together on *Majera*, and he'd never asked me to make a Friday-night *cuma*. I figured he'd invite me to pray with him before anyone else. After all, Marta and Peter's Finitism was way different from our faiths, and Pinky's spirituality, if he had any, was… alien.

Fareedh never did invite me, though. As for going through my rituals, well, I'd let my stock of Sabbath candles sit in a box in the back of my cabin's closet for the better part of the year. It was funny how you can let your faith fade even at the times it could be the greatest comfort.

Right now, I needed that comfort and a tangible link to something cherished. For a moment, I could almost imagine my mother there, reciting the Kiddush, her *tallit* draped over strong shoulders. My vision blurred, and I blinked away the sting.

The door to my cabin chimed, interrupting me mid-word. I ran a hand across my eyes and palmed the portal open.

It was Marta.

I felt my cheeks flush slightly, and my gaze flickered between her and the candles.

"It's been a while," she said, looking down at me, a sweet smile curving her lips. She added, "I mean the Sabbath."

"Yeah, well…" I swallowed. "I was just going to do the Kiddush. But, I mean, I don't have to. I mean, you probably don't want to join me, right?"

She put a soft hand on my shoulder. A dimple appeared in her round cheek. "I'd love to join you."

I felt my lips returning the smile, though they struggled. I stepped aside, gesturing her into the room.

"It's nice in here," Marta said. For once, my cabin was reasonably clean. I'd remembered to dump my old clothes in the Maker bin, and even the bed was made. Of course she'd notice.

I shrugged. "I figured I should end the week right. And there's the whole respectfulness thing, I guess."

She nodded, kneeling on the floor. I didn't have an extra chair. I sat down next to her, feeling her warmth as I stared ahead at the twin flames. Her presence seemed to fill the room.

I found myself saying, "I'm sorry I never went to any of your services."

"I never went to yours either," she said quietly. I thought I heard regret.

"Well," I cleared my throat on the word, "Here goes." I grasped the thin-stemmed cup from the table. Now I could smell the tang of grape juice, and it primed me like the first charge in a fusion chamber.

The ancient words again came from my throat, springing forth like I'd sung them every week without a break. A passage more than three thousand years old, celebrating the day of rest, honoring its creator. In a language, so far as I knew, no one in the Empire spoke in everyday life, but which few hadn't at least some acquaintance with.

For Marta, the words must be doubly meaningless. I looked up at her uncertainly, lips still framing the blessing. She was looking ahead, the expression on her freckled face relaxed, her hands folded easily in her broad lap.

My shoulders untightened, and I finished the song with clear tones.

"That's that," I said.

Her green eyes took me in, shining slightly. "I wish I'd listened to you sooner," she said.

I looked down. "I think that's my line."

She covered my hand with hers without a word. A simultaneous pang and thrill ran through my chest.

"So, what's up?" I asked at last.

Her laugh was a musical thing. "Oh, it's silly. I was thinking about Jub-Jub's planet. I feel like it needs a name."

"You're not in love with GM +156 1c?" I teased.

"It doesn't exactly roll off the tongue."

I turned to lean back against my bunk, withdrawing my hand

from Marta's. I rubbed it absently while I considered. A name…well, what defined the planet? One thing we'd noted while we were on Jub-Jub's backward DNA world is that you could eat everything that grew or swam there. It would run right through you, neither nutritious nor poisonous. If you could make it tasty, it'd make the perfect buffet for someone who didn't want to gain weight.

"We talked about making it a resort planet," I said at last. "How about 'Paradise'?"

She wrinkled her nose prettily. "You're forgetting the smell."

"Pinky liked the smell," I rejoined.

"Of course he did."

"Um…" I said, pondering. "Well, we could continue the tradition of naming planets after Sirena. Sort of, like, in honor of her."

That got a giggle. "Sirena II, the gastric revenge?"

"Okay, maybe not that. But she's got plenty of other names to spare," I said.

"How about 'Isabella'?" Marta ventured. "I like that name. It has 'beautiful' inside it."

"You don't think *that's* false advertising?"

She shrugged slightly. "It's more subtle than 'Paradise'."

"Fair enough," I conceded. I raised my glass in toast. "To Isabella." I looked at the small table, the candles now half spent. "I'm sorry I only Made one cup. I didn't know I'd have company."

"We can share," Marta said without hesitation. She leaned over, gripping the glass just above my fingers. "To Isabella," she said, then pulled the cup to her lips, my fingers still clasped around the stem. She took a sip before letting go, her eyes never leaving mine.

Thank goodness for the dim lighting. My blush would have surely stood out, even under my darker skin. Marta must have caught it anyway. She eyed me curiously. "A lira for your thoughts?"

I paused, then found myself blurting, "Marta, do Peter and Fareedh have something going on?"

Marta settled back onto her calves. She frowned as she smoothed the fabric of her skirt over her thighs.

"Do *we*?" she asked.

"You…and me?" I asked, looking up at her.

Her eyes wavered as they searched mine. "Yes. Us."

My lips parted to answer, but Marta went on. "I know it wasn't the right time before, when I came to you on our first flight. And I know we had our problems before that, when we were together." Her eyes started to shine. "But you're doing it again."

"What?" I asked, my voice a whisper.

"Avoiding me."

I tried to snort. To protest. How could I avoid her in a ship 50 meters long, half of that power plant and Drive?

She was right though.

"I'm sorry," I said. "I guess I didn't want to…you know…step on anyone's toes. It's a small ship, and we're all friends." And Marta and Peter were a thing, had been for two years. Longer than Marta and I had been a thing.

Marta put her hands on mine again. They were very warm. "We're still all friends. You don't think Peter knows?"

I felt my eyebrow quirk. "Knows..?"

She rolled her eyes, "Kitra, I've been thinking about our kiss on the *Faucon* ever since it happened. Peter was there. He saw it. He knows how I feel about you, and he's pretty sure he knows how you feel about me." Her voice softened as she followed up with, "Is he right?"

A flash of memories danced behind my eyes: Marta charging down the *Faucon's* main corridor like Achilles taking Troy, shots sizzling past her; Marta in *Faucon's* sick bay, her surgical whites smudged crimson with Fareedh's blood; the flashing lights of *Faucon's* main battery control room blinking behind Marta as we floated in air, her lips approaching mine.

Of course he was right. I managed a nod.

Marta cocked her head slightly, "So, why run away?"

"But Peter…"

She scoffed, "Peter's doing *just* fine, Kitra."

"So they *do* have something going on!"

Marta laughed merrily. "You really are oblivious, aren't you?"

"What else is new?!"

"Kitra, Peter and Fareedh have been a thing since the Émilie. I think even Sirena figured it out."

My eyes widened at that. "And you're okay with that?"

She looked at me as if it was the silliest question. "Why wouldn't I be?"

"Does…that mean you and Peter aren't…"

Marta looked at me with surprised disbelief. "Of course we are!"

I blinked. My internal *sayar* was not computing.

"Kitra," she said simply, "Do you love me?"

There was only one answer to that, for any meaning one might apply to the word.

"Yes."

She let out a breath slowly and said, "Good." Then she closed her eyes and leaned forward, the warmth of her reaching me just before her lips. The Sabbath candles guttered and smoke began to rise from their wicks, coiling toward the ventilation in the ceiling.

Marta stayed the night.

Chapter Two

Launch +36

Things were a lot better after that. We had time for a quick S&S session in the morning before Jump out, and I didn't flinch away when Marta sat next to me. Or when she made a point of holding my hand. I looked up at Peter, but he was too busy trying to succeed with his character's latest exploit to notice. Grond, his Space Barbarian, member of the fantastical warrior race of Braks, was taking on an installation of Thagmorp goons.

Peter likes to play against type.

Pinky *did* notice, however. While he described the furious hand-to-hand combat, whipping two of his hands for emphasis and using phrases like "mighty thews" and "squamous faces", one of his swirly eyespots rolled in my direction. Without missing a beat, he stretched a rough paw over my free hand. Maybe he felt left out.

Anyway, by the time Grond and his companions, Lionel the Rogue, Ukko the Blast-archer, Meryem the Blessed, and—Pinky's stand-in—Ruddy of Roccama, had thoroughly vanquished the Thagmorps, we were about as rollicking as it got. Peter was half out of his chair, waving his still-steaming '*Majera* special' pastry like a sword, proclaiming sole responsibility for the victory. Fareedh jabbed him in the ribs with the stick of the gooey *locoum* dessert he'd been nibbling on. Peter looked incredulously at him, exclaiming in a theatrical voice, "What treachery is this?! Mine own friend, Lionel, whom I trusted like family?"

I yelped in laughter.

Marta piped up with a giggle, pointing meaningfully at Fareedh's candy, "Oh I don't know, I think it's Turkish *delight*ful."

"100 Skill Points to Ukko," Pinky said without missing a beat.

It took Peter a second to get it. Then his angular face took on a pained expression. "My own girlfriend…Now *you've* got the Pinkies."

Marta blew him a kiss. "It'll happen to you too, love. It's just a matter of time."

For his part, Pinky just became more pink. Meanwhile, my over-thinking brain tried to reconcile Marta's hand on mine and her expression of affection for Peter. After running around in circles for a second, my mind just froze up entirely, and I figured, the heck with it. I was having too much fun.

It was like the old days, maybe even better.

Wiping the tears of laughter from my eyes, I stole a glance at my *sayar*. Then I jumped out of my seat.

"It's late!" I exclaimed. "We've got to take our stations."

Fareedh looked up, dropping his candy on the table. "Four minutes. Whoops!"

Pinky poofed his virtual dice out of existence and calmly added, "Failed awareness check. Last one to the bridge is a rotten potato."

I won that race, partly because I was first out of my chair, partly because I'm small enough to slide past any number of blockading limbs and pseudopods. I settled into the pilot's chair of the *Majera*, the seat adjusting to my contours, the control sticks popping out of the console. I put my hands on them as Pinky took his usual spot next to me, the rustle of fabric on chairs behind me telling of Peter and Marta's arrival. Fareedh was a blur at the edge of my vision to my right. As usual, I kept my eyes on the Window.

The panoramic screen that dominated the forward half of the bridge was off, of course. Only a loony would try experiencing hyperspace with it on. A loony like me. If Marta hadn't found me, that time I tried it months ago on that first trip from Hyvilma with Sirena, I might *still* be in that Jump-induced hallucination, wide-eyed and glued to my seat. Well, at least I hadn't tried it again.

It was tempting, though. One of these days…

Peter called out. "Levels are nominal. We've got plenty of time. Three minutes, twenty seconds."

Fareedh added, "Ship's *sayar* subsystems all check out."

"Communications and sensors standing by," Marta chimed in. "Diagnostic loops completed."

I looked over at Pinky expectantly. His swirly eyespots met my gaze.

"What?" he asked, as if surprised.

"Isn't this where you make a report?"

"Oh! Ah..." He fiddled with his panel, stubby fingers on three hands stabbing at random. "Yep! That's a panel, alright."

I shook my head, smiling. It didn't matter much, and he knew it. Either his coordinates were right, and we'd pop out in normal space somewhere near the golden sun designated GM +175, or they'd be wrong, and we'd be in the middle of nowhere. He'd never been wrong, and with Peter's magic equations, we'd have plenty of fuel even if he was. It was a strange, freeing feeling, this infinite margin for error. Our only limiting factor was food, and we had at least enough for five more weeks.

"Should I take a pill, Peter?" I asked, looking over at him. He was seated behind me.

He shrugged broad shoulders. "Did you need them last time?"

That was another bit of surreality. Virtually every time I'd gone into Jump, and I'd done it a lot, both on *Majera* and before that, on mom's ship, *L' Emmisaire*, that transition into and out of hyperspace had been savagely, if briefly, painful. They'd been like the awful cramps I'd endured every month before my 14th birthday made me eligible for the Shot. But on both of the last Jumps, only Peter's words, *Majera's* instrumentation, and once, a brief flicker I'd figured was automatic circuits dimming the bridge lighting, had shown we'd made a transition from one kind of space to another. No cramps.

Again, I felt that pang, the idea that, by giving up this secret, we'd lose something special. I shook my head to loosen myself of the feeling. Peter took it as a simple response to his question and nodded in satisfaction, a proud smile creasing his face.

"Two minutes," Fareedh said after a quiet moment. "Anyone want to make bets?"

"On the system?" Marta asked. "It's got a pretty wide biosphere. Five planets, no gas giants. I'm going to be optimistic and say three inhabitable worlds."

Pinky made a good approximation of a scoffing sound. Of course, he could approximate virtually any sound. His whole body was a nose, a mouth, and everything else. "Planet One is going to be a cinder or a sauna," he said. "Three is going to be an ice ball. So I'll bet one world. No need to be greedy."

"I'll follow that and raise you," Peter said. "I don't think there will be any inhabitable planets. Then we'll just have to go home, and I can write my papers."

"Ah, Grond the Courageous," Fareedh murmured. "And here I thought the party was just getting started. I'll say two, just to be contrarian. Kitra?" His dark eyes sought mine as I turned to face him. I couldn't help smiling. He really was a pretty, pretty man.

"Seven thousand — might as well blow the stack," I said, exhausting my knowledge of poker terms, at least in French. I knew some more in Turkish, but I was done with the metaphor.

"Phew!" Pinky said with a whistle. "I hope I'm with you on *that* flight."

I glanced at the countdown display. "We'll know in fifteen seconds."

With that, I put on my business face, grabbing the sticks and giving "The Tree" a quick once-over. The branching set of readouts at the center of the console was a myriad of green: power plant, engines, life systems, comm laser, all were in fine shape. The Drive light glowed brightly with activation. Only the multi-use pod indicator was brown; we still didn't have one. The last of Sirena's commission, what she'd paid us to find the world named after her and bring her back, had barely covered repairs and maintenance. This was going to be our last trip for a while unless we could find another client. Well, it was going to be our last trip together, regardless. Peter and Marta were going back to school after this. I shook my head slightly. I didn't want to think about it.

"Egress," Peter said, pulling me out of myself.

There was a brief flash, and for the barest moment the ship seemed to vanish, leaving me hanging in an infinite field of gray. No, not gray, a void beyond color. I squeezed my eyes shut, and there was a green glow behind my eyelids, already fading. My first thought was that the

Window had turned on prematurely, but as I opened my eyes again, the screen was just snapping to life.

"Did anyone else see that?" I asked in a croak. I looked over at the others. Fareedh shrugged, and Marta cocked her head quizzically.

"See what?" Peter asked.

"Never mind," I said quickly. There weren't even after-images. Had this ever happened before? Certainly not on *L'émissaire*, nor before Peter had come up with the super-Drive. I tried to remember that wild Jump back to Hyvilma, when we'd first used the super-Drive technique to escape the pirates, but all I could recall was worry for Pinky. Besides this one, there had been four Jump-ins and Jump-outs since: from Hyvilma to the colony of Son Duryak, from Son Duryak to Pureté (avoiding the nasty Puritans who were squatting there), Pureté to Sirena, Sirena to Isabella.

I pursed my lips in thought. No, I was sure the flicker had never happened before in all the prior Jumps.

"Um, Kitra?" Pinky urged me hesitantly.

I coughed and quickly turned my attention back to the Window. The white-sparkled panorama in the display made the cramped bridge suddenly feel much more spacious, an island in a sea of stars. Reflexively, I gripped the controls, my muscles tight as I strained my ears for the collision alarm which had never sounded since we'd started flying in *Majera*. It didn't make sense I would hear it now, either. Certainly, I couldn't expect to find another ship here in the vastness of unexplored space, and the odds of a wayward rock being anywhere nearby were vanishingly low. And yet, here I was, my tightly curled fingers cold pressed against sticks as they wicked away their sweat.

The yellow blaze of GM +175 came into view, the Window automatically dimming it to a tolerable brightness. From the span of its disk, it was clear Pinky had dropped us in the inhabitable zone, maybe 150 million kilometers out. Just as I was making that mental calculation, displays popped up in the Window confirming that and telling more. Two rings appeared around a central point, showing two planets around the star, each labeled with further details.

Pinky started reading them off as they showed up. "It looks like we will have an answer to our inhabitable planets wager soon. Two of the five planets confirmed, 128 million kilometers and 158 million kilometers from primary." A third ring popped into place as *Majera's* sensors caught the light of another world and measured its velocity. "Whoops. Make that three planets confirmed. 195 M-KM for that one." Their orbital tracks were refining even as I watched. This was becoming my favorite part of exploring stars: watching the ship's *sayar* piece together a system from pinpoints of light. It was like magic.

I watched the inner two points closely. From our last vantage point, several parsecs away, all we could see was the wiggle of GM +175 caused by the gravity of its family of planets. We had only a vague idea of their masses and none whatsoever about what they were like. In a few minutes, *Majera's* systems would have a complete analysis of their reflected sunshine, reading their spectra like fingerprints.

"Clear on all normal comm channels," Marta said. "No transponders or traffic."

I looked back and grinned. "We're the first ones here?"

Peter intercepted my gaze, physically placing himself between me and Marta to answer, "That's what we thought when the pirates jumped us."

Fareedh scuffed him from his seat with his sandaled foot. His legs were *long*. "Don't be a killjoy. Besides, 107 was a charted fueling spot. This is the far end of nowhere."

"Not to also be a killjoy," Pinky broke in, "but we're 50 M-KM from Number One and 12 from Number Two. We'd hardly pick up low energy planetary traffic from here." He clucked reprovingly. "We aren't the only beings in the galaxy."

I flushed slightly. He was right. It was too easy to think of the Frontier in terms of human expansion, not taking into account who else might be out here. After all, there were Pinky's people and the Bugs, not to mention the Grilchies, who had ships, kind of. And there were the ruins of a starfaring culture Helmi Kader had found on Talvi…

"Why did you park us so far out?" Peter wanted to know.

Pinky's shrug was three-shouldered. "I didn't know which planet we'd want to inspect first. And with fuel not an issue, I opted for minimum chance of collision and maximum ease of access. You'll note that we're headed straight for Two, but it will take only the gentlest nudge to send us to One *or* Three." He paused expectantly, clearly wanting praise.

I gave it to him. "You're a genius, Pinky," I said, patting a rubbery arm.

"It's true!"

"Speaking of geniuses," Peter said, turning to look at Marta, "Do we have spectra? I want to know who won the bet."

"I was just about to mention," she replied, catching Fareedh's eye and then waggling her eyebrows in his signature fashion. "If you want to stretch a point, you win the bet."

"Come again?" Fareedh drawled.

Rectangular rainbows popped up on the Window in the planetary display, segmented with thin black lines. They didn't mean much to me, but Marta could read them quite clearly.

"Number Two has got a strong O2 line, and Number One's isn't far behind," she went on. "Number Two has got a mass of 1.1e and a surface gravity of 1.05g. Number One's at .8e and .9g. I can't tell you air pressure yet, not without some soundings, but just looking at the cloud heights, I'd say they won't be too far off standard."

Fareedh smugly curled his legs under him in his chair and leaned back with an ostentatious sigh.

Pinky snapped, "You haven't won yet. What's the blackbody temperature of Number One, not to mention if it's got a greenhouse going? It's probably too hot to count as inhabitable."

"Hey, weren't you the one who said we need to think beyond humanity in terms of planets?" Fareedh teased.

Pinky's skin flushed yellow with disapproval. "We should have clarified terms before we made bets." His tone edged close to a whine.

I looked at Pinky with worry. He never got upset over silly things like this. Fareedh also picked up on his discomfort. He leaned forward and gave his center shoulder a squeeze. "Why don't we call it a tie?"

The yellow quickly vanished. "I'm sorry," Pinky said sheepishly. "I don't know what got into me."

I had a suspicion. That sounded like some of L' éclair's stiff collar seeping through. It must have been harder to keep the Lieutenant's personality distinct from his own when Pinky was under stress. I scrambled to think of a good fart joke. That'd snap him back into shape.

But Marta was talking again, "Folks, I'm reading some weird peaks in Number Two's spectrum. Sulfur dioxide, nitrogen oxides, and a few other chemicals."

I looked my question at her. My understanding of chemistry mostly extended to making acid-and-bicarb fizz bombs.

She crinkled her forehead adorably. "It *could* be natural. Volcanoes make SO2. Lightning makes nitrogen oxides."

"You don't sound convinced," Peter said.

"Well, they could also be from power generation."

I frowned, confused. "How do you get…those gases from power plants? All fusion makes is helium."

"You can get power from burning things, too," Marta explained.

"Seriously?"

"What about those rocket-ships you read about in your romances?" Fareedh asked.

"For reaction motors, sure. But on a planetary scale?" I had visions of a civilization running on a million beach party fire pits. "That sounds ridiculous."

"A lot of the Midworlds did it," Peter said. "If their fusion plant broke down, they had to burn local fuel. Fossilized plants."

That sounded unpleasant. Wood smoke left a stench in my hair until I could wash it out. Imagine a planet covered with the stuff!

Then the full impact of what Marta and Peter were saying hit me. "You mean, these signatures could mean…people?"

Marta's eyes glowed. She nodded. "Some kind of people, anyway."

"Like a rogue colony," Fareedh suggested. He nodded toward Pinky and added, "or aliens."

"Stink-producing aliens. My kind of people."

I smiled. That was the Pinky I knew.

"I can't imagine a human colony this far out," I said, "not reaching this distance *and* falling back on burning stuff for power."

Three alien races known to humanity. Were we about to discover the fourth?

I licked my lips. "Pinky," I said, "lay in a course for Planet Two."

"Aye, aye, Cap'n. ETA is 15 hours at 2g."

Chapter Three

Launch +37

I blew the steam off my second cup of coffee and took a scalding sip. It was Maker-made, and probably a bad idea this late at night, but none of us could sleep, now that we were here. If chance dictated that history would be made in the middle of the night, well, that's the way it was. So I gulped the mediocre stuff and waited for the buzz. At least Pinky had gotten a nap. I thought about getting Jub-Jub out of its terrarium so I could pet it and have something to do with my hands.

"Definitely artificial," Marta called from behind me.

Okay, *now* I was awake! I took a deep breath, willing my heart to relax. Jub-Jub would have to wait.

"Surface pressure's 136 kilopascals," she went on, "almost like back home. The atmosphere goes up about as high as on Vatan, too. Based on that, I'd say anthropogen…er…sorry Pinky, *technogenic* gasses make up more than half of the spikes I found. There's just no way the weather or tectonics is active enough to make so much, and on all those wavelengths at once. Kitra…" I looked over my shoulder at her, and her eyes were glowing. "There's people there. Some kind of people."

"Wild," Fareedh breathed. I looked over at him and I saw his lips set in an almost manic smile. "The Bugs and Pinky's people weren't anywhere near spaceflight when we met them, and the Grilchies already had it. If these beings are burning fossil fuels, they must be right on the cusp."

"Assuming everybody develops like we did," Peter countered. "And who knows? Maybe this is their equivalent of a Midworld."

"Maybe we should…" Marta and Pinky said at the same time. Pinky extended a pseudopod and said, "Sorry, go ahead."

I swiveled my chair around to see everyone. Marta smiled and said, "I was going to say, maybe we should power up the comm laser. Just in case."

"Yeah, that's what I was going to say," Pinky agreed.

I frowned. "Really? Go in guns ready? Isn't that a bad way to make a first impression?"

Pinky spread out all three hands in a kind of shrug. "After the pirates, I'm inclined toward caution, despite my pacifist nature," he said. "Besides, we're just making sure its capacitor is charged. That won't be detectable, and in any event, it's a comm laser."

"Yeah," Peter said with a nod. "The whole reason you let us have it is because it serves double duty."

"Fine," I said, trying to keep the irritation out of my voice. They were right. I just rejected guns on principle. Having to use them on the *Faucon* hadn't warmed me up to them any. I took a deep breath, willing myself to calm down, but the caffeine jitters were already settling in.

Fareedh seemed to catch my mood, and he shifted the subject. "Marta? Anything on the comms? We should be close enough, yeah?"

She shook her head, curls jiggling. "Nothing on our main bands. Nothing on conventional frequencies. We're still about half a mega out, though."

I looked back at the Tree. The comm system glowed green.

As if reading my thoughts, Marta said, "It's working, silly. If it makes you feel better, when we get close enough, I'll be able to hear natural phenomena like lightning flashes and whistlers to prove our comm systems are fine. But I'm sure we'll catch something before that." There was the excitement of hope in her voice.

Majera continued its course toward Two, facing backward as the ship's engines blasted at two gees of constant deceleration. As we traveled, I kept my mind busy thinking about possible names for the planet; we'd have to come up with something better than 'Two'. Another Sirena-inspired name? Bits of the Spanish Sirena had taught us when she had been on board bounced around my foggy brain, but without knowing more about our destination, nothing jumped out as fitting. In any event, if the planet was inhabited, they'd have their own name for it.

Probably their version of 'Earth'.

Pinky's course had us headed into orbit about 200 kilometers high. Luckily, there were no moons to complicate the gravitational dance, though that would have been only a minor inconvenience for him and the ship's *sayar*. Over time, less than an hour, but it felt like a day, our destination grew from a small disk to fill the Window. Now it was a world, a real, breathing planet, turning under us, the horizon gently curved and glowing.

And a beautiful world at that. There were vast oceans of blue and an expanse of brown land ridged with sharp slopes, crested with shiny white. Whorls of clouds dappled the globe. It reminded me of planet Sirena, not green tinted like Vatan or purplish like Hyvilma. The atmospheric spectra still registered the oxygen of life, the hydrocarbons of primitive industry. Surely there was someone here. Yet, the whole way, and even now, Marta reported no communications. Maybe Marta had been wrong after all?

At last, our ship backed into orbit around Two, and the engines went off. There was no accompanying change in gravity—*Majera's* antigrav could handle a lot more than two gees. I thought I noticed a lack of a background rumble, but it might have been my imagination. In any event, the instruments were what mattered, and they said our only acceleration now was angular, an orbiting free-fall around the planet that wouldn't change until we changed it ourselves.

Marta made an odd sound, somewhere between a 'hmm' and an 'eep'. We all turned to look at her. She made a shushing gesture, her head tilted as if toward a noise. She must have had her private comms going, listening to sounds we couldn't hear. Out of the corner of my eye, I saw Pinky start quietly working his own panel.

Finally, Marta looked up. "There's something going on. I've caught a few high frequency bands that are active, and also some beeps up around 2 Gigahertz."

"The beeps sound like satellites," Pinky added quickly. A moment later, he followed up with, "Yeah, I've got doppler on them." Pinky beat a quick tattoo on his panel, and several sub-displays popped up, each with gleaming, jagged objects, fuzzy with distance, in their centers. They could have been satellites; they didn't look like rocks. "Now that I'm looking," Pinky said, "I can see more of them. Not many, though, and most aren't transmitting."

Satellites! I cleared my throat. "You said there are active bands, Marta?"

Lines furrowed her forehead. "Well yeah, sort of. Too faint to get a fix on. Something's broadcasting, filling the band locally, but not saying anything. Like someone left a transmitter on, but all we're getting is the carrier wave without any actual signal to carry information."

"Another ghost planet?" Fareedh said, almost too low to hear.

"Abandoned, you think? Like Jaiyk?" Peter asked.

I shivered, remembering that ocean planet with its empty military base and its poisonous air. It had been our very first destination with *Majera*, and not a planned stop.

"I hope so," I replied. "I can deal with empty a lot better than I can with dead."

"You know," Peter said, not entirely succeeding at keeping his tone light, "we could raise our altitude a bit and do a wide-angle sweep with the deep radar."

"I don't want to spook them if they *are* there. The less we broadcast, the better, at least for now," I said, turning back to the window. "We'll make landfall soon enough."

As if on cue, the first blurred bits of coastline slid over the horizon. I leaned forward in my seat and squinted. It was a clear day as we made landfall. At first, the ground looked untouched and natural: the rumpled brown of mountains, brownish-green valleys, a fine gray network of rivers, the sun the wrong angle to reflect off of them. I amped up the magnification, and my breath caught. Impossibly straight lines that couldn't be natural waterways came into view, linking sprawling, pebbly clusters of white and gray. Most tellingly, I saw swaths of sharp-edged green spaces that had to be crop fields, but not circular, like the ones we had on Vatan. If the satellites hadn't given things away, the view did. This was definitely an inhabited world!

I looked over at the velocity display. We were doing nearly 8 kilometers per second. Already, the coastline was behind us, and the wrinkled terrain of the continent spread out ahead of us. The straight lines criss-crossed the ground as far as I could see. This wasn't a recently colonized planet. People, some kind of people, had been here for hundreds, maybe thousands of years. My heart began to race.

It couldn't be Imperials. I was sure of that. A colony ship from the Core couldn't have gotten this far out so long ago as to develop such a civilization. Those short ranged ships of the first century of starflight couldn't have made it even as far as Vatan. They certainly couldn't have crossed the starless five-parsec Rift that separated Punnainen and Hyvilma to settle in the Frontier.

Maybe there had been an accident that had flung a colony ship farther than we knew was possible. No, if something like that had happened in the seven hundred years of interstellar travel, surely it'd be common knowledge by now. In any event, the odds of such a freak accident landing a ship near a star, much less one with an inhabitable world, was vanishingly small. I was sure we were the first humans to visit this place. Unless…

As I watched the green and beige plains rise into the stark-shadowed peaks of a mountain range, puffy clouds pressed against the seaward side, another thought came to me. It had been centuries since anyone had heard from Earth. Maybe the planets in the Core Worlds of the Empire, dozens of light years from Vatan and closest to Earth, had some kind of contact with the original birthplace of humanity. But I'd grown up with the sense that Earth had sort of walled themselves off from everyone. Maybe that was wrong. Maybe they'd developed some kind of super-drive and leapfrogged us.

I called up a starmap, sectioning off a bit of the Window, then slid the scale to display the explored part of the galaxy. It wasn't much space compared to the entirety of the Milky Way, but it was still at least a hundred light years across. Seen from overhead, our sprawling Empire looked a bit like a slice of pie. The inner tip was the Core Worlds, and the settled stars collectively called the Midworlds spread out in a widening triangle until they reached the Frontier, which made the crust. Vatan was near that crust, a little orange light near the brighter point that was Sennet, the provincial capital world. Punnainen and Hyvilma were at opposite sides of the Rift that formed the outer border of the crust.

Not for the first time, I wondered why the Empire had spread the way it had. Why hadn't humanity expanded in a circle? I knew some of the answer — the Grilchies formed part of one of the edges of the pie. They'd been a barrier to expansion for as long as I could remember, too alien to talk terms with. But that was just one section. What was on the other side? How about the opposite side?

"Been a while since I looked at a map that scale," Fareedh commented.

"Yeah," I said. "I was just thinking. Could these people be human, but from outside the Empire?"

"You mean like the Shinjeh legends?" Peter asked, mangling the word, Çince. They'd been one of the main people of Earth, but hardly represented in the Empire. There were rumors that they had their own nation somewhere among the stars, them and the Desi, the latter of whom I knew had also settled at least one of the Midworlds.

"Maybe," I said. "I guess we can ask Shari if she knows anything about them next time we're on Sirena. I'm pretty sure Chang is a Çince name."

Past the mountains, the planetscape was a tremendous network of rivers, fields, darker patches that might have been swampland, and more of those tantalizing straight lines, coming together at those pebbly nodes like diagrams of neurons from high school biology. Now we were coming to an enormous plain, green with cultivation, an endless expanse of faint-bordered squares and rectangles. Again, there was the sense that this had all grown up over time, rather than spreading from one or a few colony ships. Even if one of the old giant people-movers from half a millennium ago had gotten out here by some freak accident, there was no way they could have populated an entire continent so quickly.

The land mass continued into the twilight terminator, the horizon fading to black. As *Majera* slid toward the planet's night, there was an unnerving twinge in the back of my mind, but I couldn't quite place why. Something unnatural about the view.

"No lights," Marta said. The words hung in the air.

That was it. With all the signs of civilization, the landscape should have been lit up like the night sky. But it was completely, ominously dark.

"If they're aliens," Pinky said calmly, "maybe they don't use the visible wavelength."

"Fair point," Marta said. "I should have thought of that." There was a pause, and all I heard was the soft whir of the ventilation fans and the sounds of our breathing. Then, "But it's dark all over the spectrum," she added.

"What do you mean?" I asked.

"Aside from those signals I talked about earlier, there's nothing. Aside from no lights, I'm also not picking up anything in infrared. If they were generating power, or there's traffic, or industry, or anything, I should see something."

"Even from this high up?" Peter asked, a little incredulous.

"Even this high up. Unless everything is completely decentralized and their cars are super-efficient, but that wouldn't match all the pollutants in the air."

The fingertips and thumb of my right hand began to slide nervously against each other. I clenched them around a flight stick to keep them steady.

Forty minutes later, we were back in the light, over ocean again. In another forty minutes, we'd finish a full circuit of the planet. It wouldn't give us a complete map, not at this altitude, but we'd have a decent handle on most of the world. Then we could pick out spots of interest to survey more closely.

A set of islands came into view, small and feathery. I zoomed in on a few. There was what looked like an artificial harbor on one of them. At least, its boundaries seemed too regular to be natural. There were no tracks of shipping traffic, though we might be too high to see. That's what I told myself.

Then we were over another continent, this one narrow at first, like the tip of a spear, but as we flew over the ridge that made its shaft, it quickly expanded. Once more, there was the telltale mottling of gray and green, interspersed with the white of clouds. If there was a difference between the pattern of settlement on this side of the planet versus the other, I couldn't tell.

"I'm getting those empty bands again," Marta said. "Faint, but something is definitely broadcasting."

"They couldn't be natural, could they?" That was Fareedh.

Pinky answered for Marta, "Then they'd be static. These are being swept clear by the carrier waves."

"What he said," Marta added, her smile tingeing her voice.

The second landmass slowly passed beneath us. Like the first continent, there was no part of it that wasn't at least sparsely settled. The only times I didn't see civilization was when we passed over a stretch of beige desert. Otherwise, there was the same network of lines and nodes, more cultivation. This time, I noted, the fields *were* round like back home. While I looked at the scenery, Peter went back to the wardroom to get us some food, coming back with a tray of *Majera* specials and cups of water. I nibbled at mine absently as the opposite coastline came into view. Soon, we were back over open water.

"Well, what do we do now?" Fareedh asked. He was looking at me, and he knew what the answer had to be.

"I guess we take a closer look," I said. Again, that shiver up my spine, part from excitement, and just a little part from fear. I checked the fuel display: 88%. Plenty to spare for an expensive maneuver, especially with all the free water below that could be turned into fuel. I turned the ship around and fired the engines, at the same time angling the grav thrusters down to keep us from losing altitude as we decelerated. I wanted to come down near the shoreline so we didn't have to waste time backtracking.

Once our orbital velocity was zero, it was just the thrusters keeping us up. I reduced them, and we began to descend, slowly and gently, like a balloon with a slow leak, the way most modern ships landed. The days of fiery, unpowered reentry were long behind us. I smiled ruefully at that, remembering that I'd actually made two such landings in the last years, but those had been under special circumstances.

Just fifteen minutes later, we were hovering a few thousand meters above the ocean, rippled and glistening like the skin of a fish. It reminded me of the sea off Denizli, Vatan's capital, though as if through some kind of blue filter. That made it seem colder, somehow. Sterile.

I pressed forward on the sticks. We'd come down about 200 kilometers offshore. As had been the case on the continent's opposite shore, we came across a line of islands first, craggy and seemingly uninhabited. I gauged them to be about 150 kilometers away, turning the horizon into a series of lumpy peaks.

"I've got something!" Marta said in a relieved gust. "X Band, directional. Someone's sending us a message, I think."

Pinky tinged toward ochre. I looked over in concern. "What is it?" I asked.

"Nobody sends messages on X Band," he said simply.

"Folks," Fareedh spoke up. "I'm getting a heat signature from one of the islands."

I tensed. "A beam?"

"It's a reaction drive, pulling five gees and increasing."

Peter's voice was puzzled, "A welcoming committee?"

"Eight gees," Fareedh continued.

"No," Pinky said, answering Peter. "An interceptor."

Inside a new display, I saw a fuzzy, pointy-ended cylinder, flame streaking out the back. It looked like a firework, not a vessel.

"Is there anyone on board the thing?" I called out.

"Don't think so," Pinky replied evenly. "It's only a ton in mass."

"A missile," I spat out. "Can we shoot it down?" My aversion to guns had an exception. A pirate torpedo had nearly cooked *Majera* just a few weeks before, and I wasn't about to let this one get anywhere near us.

Fareedh nodded in my peripheral vision. "It's on a ballistic course."

Pinky's voice went flat, "Hit it now. It's probably got a warhead."

"You don't have to tell me twice." I touched the comm laser controls and set the target, picked the highest frequency beam it allowed — well into the ultraviolet — then overrode the limiters: this was a message I wasn't interested in getting a reply to.

The beam had no recoil, of course, and it was invisible. But moments later, the missile was a shower of sparks quickly fading to ashes.

"Any more of those things?" I asked, ready to open up the grav thrusters to give us some quick altitude if we needed it, never mind the fuel use.

"Nothing," Fareedh said.

The bulk of the continent was visible past the islands now. We'd be over the shore in a matter of minutes. "You were saying?" I asked without turning to look at Pinky, my tone sharp. "What's the X Band used for?"

"Ground-based, missile defense radars. At least, before deep radar," he explained. Out of the corner of my eye, I saw him flush maroon. "Sorry I didn't make it clearer. Sometimes L' éclair's stuff is hard to access."

"You did great, Pinky," I said, willing my voice to mellow. I took a hand off the stick long enough to pat his head.

"So what do we do now?" Peter asked. "Just sail over their whole network and hope they don't send more than one at a time? The capacitor only charges so fast."

"Marta, are you still getting hit on the X Band?" I asked.

"Not anymore," she said. "The clear bands are getting stronger, though."

"The ones broadcasting dead air?"

"Yes, carrier waves only."

I rubbed my chin then shook my head in a short jerk. "You know what? They know we're here. Peter, get ready to do an emergency Jump if we need to, and I'll hit thrusters *and* engines at full blast if anything comes at us." I paused, then said, "Pinky, engage the deep radar."

"Aye aye, cap'n."

I gripped the sticks, feeling a bit giddy. Any other captain in the universe would be completely loonie to consider Jumping so close to a planet. The rule I'd learned was that the safe zone *started* at five diameters from a planet's center. Trying to enter hyperspace from any closer made a ship end up like the Émilie, or worse. But now, from what Peter and Fareedh had figured out, there *was* no minimum limit. Heck, Peter might be able to figure out a way to do it from a planet's surface — if he could be persuaded to try. If *I* could. It was probably a job for a robot to test, not us.

The view through the Window transformed. Above the horizon, the sky was flat gray, and the ocean below a deep slate. The shoreline now was bright yellow and orange. I knew if we focused the deep radar below, we could scan through the water and map the contours of the sea floor, but that wasn't what I was looking for.

We were near enough now that we could see more and more inland, and in the stark light of the deep radar this close to the ground, those tantalizing hints of civilization became crystal clear, dots and splotches of blue mottled virtually all of the terrain, with dark lanes between them.

"Towns," Fareedh said simply.

"And roads," Pinky added.

Marta chimed in, "Still no communications. Nothing on X band."

In the weird wavelengths of the deep radar, civilization spread out in a glowing blue network. This wasn't just a set of towns, it was a metropolis. I hadn't realized how big it was from orbit.

I scanned the skies. If this were Vatan, there'd be a swarm of blue motes over the city, reflections off metal and plastic of air cars and planes. Here, there was nothing but gray.

"No air traffic," I said.

"Yeah," Pinky agreed.

"Maybe they're all grounded. Or they use high speed trains," Peter suggested.

After a moment, I added, "Let me see it in visual again," not wanting to give up the sticks to do it myself. Pinky obliged, and the sight of endless streets and buildings in natural light — a sprawl of tan and slate in straight lines and smooth arcs — was a bit intimidating. There was also something subtly wrong with the shape of the city, the way it was laid out, the shape of the buildings, the curve of the roads. Nothing that immediately said "inhuman" to the eye, but it kept pinging at my hindbrain anyway. We crossed the shoreline and still nothing shot at us. Up ahead the city faded to smaller towns and large-scale agriculture.

"Nothing's moving down there," Pinky said.

He turned up the magnification on the Window, and the city shimmered slightly, blurred by distance. From here, we should have seen cars, or trains, or…something. The subtle writhing of a living city. Anybody who builds structures has to have ways to go between them, and we were close enough to see them. Maybe not to see individuals, but there should have been something. And where was the smoke from the power plants?

Marta was speaking, "I've pinpointed a broadcast. It's coming from right below us. Still blank."

"Still nothing coming after us," Fareedh said.

"Still no welcoming committee besides that one," I said. "And from the looks of things, no one to fire it."

"Maybe an automatic," Fareedh mused.

Peter sounded dubious. "An air defense that shoots at any random ship that flies over?"

I looked over at Fareedh, who tilted his head in a shrug. "Maybe one that takes the wrong path."

"That's a pretty hair-trigger attitude," Peter said.

Marta cut in, "I'm kind of afraid to keep sailing across open sky like this."

She was right. I dropped our forward velocity to zero. No need to trip any more radars. Without taking my hands off the sticks, I said, "Well, let's go over the options. They aren't doing anything right now. Either they're all hiding, or something weird is going on." I took a deep breath, trying not to think about what that weirdness might be. "If we want to know what's happening, we're going to have to get even closer."

"You mean land?" Peter asked, an edge to his voice, "After what just happened?"

"Well, it's either that or keep scouting and maybe run into another radar." I said.

"Or go home. Let the Empire send a real contact team."

Peter had a point. This was a finding like no other. An entire world, maybe an alien world, and something was *wrong*. Maybe it was something innocent like abandonment. Maybe it was something terrible like a planet wide blackout. Were we really the best ones to deal with this? Could we? And we'd already been shot at once.

"There might have been an epidemic," Marta said, her voice grave. I added that to the list of explanations.

"Prudence dictates that we leave," Pinky said. He flushed hot pink. "But I kind of want to see what's going on. I want to meet these people. I don't want to read about this in someone else's report."

"If that report is even ever published," Fareedh said.

"Yeah!"

That was how I felt, too. We might have found aliens! But there was something else, now that Marta's words were sinking in.

"Folks," I said, "we're kind of *obligated* to check it out. If we go back, it'll take weeks, and it could be months or years before this is investigated. Maybe too late to help the people here if they need it. Remember, if we'd gone back after finding the Émilie, they probably all would have died."

"These guys might *already* be dead," Peter pointed out. "And anyway, what can five people do with," he waved his hand in a sweeping gesture at the landscape, "all that?"

"We'll never know if we leave," Marta said gently. "The ship's *sayar* has got centuries of medical knowledge in it. If there is an epidemic, we might be able to stop it."

Fareedh chuckled ruefully. "Just make sure we don't get it."

"That's what suits are for," Pinky said. With a sigh. He hated suits.

I looked over at Peter, my eyebrows going up in silent appeal. He stared back, blue eyes reflexively defiant. Finally, he threw up his hands. "Alright. Let's do another ridiculously dangerous thing again. Why stop now?" His expression softened. "And you're right. This is a really big deal."

I couldn't help but smile at that. "Okay then," I said and turned back to the controls, looking for a place to land. Now that we were committed, some of my enthusiasm had faded. Dread, urgency, and excitement replaced them, wrestling inside me to make my stomach and chest both a little topsy-turvy. Every time I thought we couldn't get any further over our heads, there we went.

But if people needed our help, especially if there was a deadline, I couldn't let them down.

Chapter Four

Our little airlock was pretty cramped with two people in it. I could only imagine how cozy it got when it was Peter and Marta checking out each other's suits. This time, it was me and Marta. In the close space, she was never more than half a meter from me, and her nearness helped me, if only for the moment, forget what all was waiting for us past the outer door when we cycled it. She patted my butt for the third time, and now I was pretty sure she wasn't just smoothing wrinkles.

"We're never going to get out of here if you keep doing that."

"You're in a hurry now?" she said, her eyes dancing.

I shook my head, smiling. "An entire world, maybe an alien world, is waiting for us out there, and you want to make out?"

"Priorities," she said. Marta put her hands on my shoulders and leaned in to kiss me. I didn't resist. I did the opposite of resisting. I pressed into her, the skin of the suit insulating me from all of her warmth except her lips and her breath. Everything faded away: the silent planet, the worries about our super drive, the ship's log that was now three days behind. It was just me and her. Perfection.

Pinky's baritone rang through the comms, "Um, ladies, we sort of need to use the lock."

I jerked, falling backward into the still-open suit rack. Marta fell too, but forward, and caught herself with her palms against the wall before she could squash me.

"We're just finishing up!" I growled. "For goodness sake, we haven't been in here that long." I looked up at Marta. "Have we?"

Her wrinkled nose and rolled eyes told me what she cared about time. She was all business after that, though. I sphered my helmet, and she made sure the seal was tight; then I did the same for her. We each hooked up an oxygen tank to the other's back. It didn't matter that there was oxygen in the air outside—who knew what germs or toxins might be floating around out there?

The suit readout said I was airtight. I faced away from the inner door, gripped Marta's gloved hand in mine, and cycled the outer lock.

Light streamed in. It was a gorgeous day outside, all blue skies with just a few wisps of high clouds. It was funny how quickly I'd gotten used to azure when I'd grown up most of my life with emerald. Maybe it was all the traveling I'd done as a kid, or the trips I'd taken recently. I briefly considered changing the wardroom ceiling to blue, as we stepped down onto the plaza that was our impromptu landing pad in the heart of the alien city, close to where Marta had pinpointed the clear broadcast. Then I wasn't thinking about decorations anymore.

The city was…empty.

Plants sprouted from cracks in the dark stone blocks of the pavement, and from the soil and debris that filled the curb ringing the empty, flat forum I'd landed *Majera* in. Scraps of cloth fluttered, their edges snatched by the breeze. It wasn't ruined, like Honaz, the town the first colonists had built on Vatan before they moved to the planned capital city of Denizli. It wasn't even like the abandoned base we'd seen on Jaiyk, battered by nearly a century of weathering. As I looked around the plaza, taking in the brown buildings that flanked it, the weird sculptures at its far end, the absolute quiet except for the whisper of the wind against my helmet, the place reminded me most of the old football field in back of the secondary school all of us except Fareedh had gone to. After the new one had been built, the old one had lain fallow for a couple of years before they built houses there. Untended, the bleachers slowly fading. That's what this felt like, up to and including the light mottling on the building walls that suggested unevenly faded paint.

"You think they just up and left, all of a sudden?" I wondered aloud, working to keep my voice steady.

Marta replied, "There's no damage. No radiation."

The mention of radiation made me glance nervously at my display, but of course, it still registered normal background levels, consistent with what we'd measured on *Majera*.

"There's plants, too," I noted.

"And animals. Look." Marta pointed overhead at a flock of somethings soaring lazily overhead. They looked like gliders, thin bodies in the middle of broad, oval membranes with tapered ends. The shimmering magenta of their forms contrasted sharply with the dirty browns of the city proper. I unclipped a grippy from my belt and plucked at a tattered piece of fabric on the ground, about the size of a shawl. At first, I thought it was some kind of disposable bag or wrapping. On closer inspection, I saw that it was finely textured with a subtle, woven pattern, actually quite beautiful. But it was a nondescript gray, clearly made from unbleached threads.

"Look at this one," Marta said. She was using her boot to spread out something the color of charcoal. It was stained and water-spotted, but fully intact, and it had several large holes with hemmed edges. "I think it's a shirt."

I grabbed it at its largest opening and held it up. The garment sagged around my grippy like a limp flag. Marta used her grippy to help spread it out. It might be a shirt. For a big person with weirdly shaped shoulders.

"Laundry day," came Fareedh's voice, both bright in my ears over comms and slightly muffled through the helmet.

"Or someone's clothes Maker exploded." That was Pinky. I dropped my end of the garment and turned back to face the ship. Fareedh's suit was a welcome splash of color, all rainbows as usual. Pinky's was white, with a big clear pane for his eyespots, and a utility belt clipped around his middle. He came up to me with an almost dainty three-legged trot. "Spooky. Why do we always find the spooky ones?"

My dry throat stung as I swallowed. "Where's the signal coming from?"

Marta swung with her *sayar*, spinning full around before settling on a general direction, then oscillating back and forth like an analog compass. Marta stood out vividly in her bright green against the dingy tans and browns.

"By the sculptures, I think," she answered. "It's hard to be sure since the signal's so strong, but it might be coming from the building behind them."

"Let's go check them out," I said. I needed something to focus on, torn between unraveling this mystery and darting back inside the ship where it was safe.

There were five sculptures, all made out of some kind of shiny stone different from whatever made up the pavement, with subtle, smooth edges. To my eye, they were there to be art rather than functional. Someone, or several someones, with real talent had made them. Three of them were incomprehensible, abstract art I didn't understand, with corkscrews and intricate geometries that made my eyes hurt to look at them. Another looked a bit like the flying creatures we'd just seen, only with a bunch of grasping tentacles.

The fifth...

"That's an alien," Marta said.

It could hardly be anything else. Five meters tall, it was sort of humanoid, if you had a loose definition of the term. There were two thick legs and a pair of arms, but the hips were too high, the limbs had three joints, and the head was a sphere. At first, I thought it might be a helmet, but there were subtle features etched into the stone, a collection of circles and indentations in a configuration that wasn't remotely human. Somehow, I knew it wasn't an abstraction, either. Was this a statue of one of the planet's people? I frowned, remembering the shirt we'd found, trying to fit it to the figure's configuration.

That's when it really hit me.

We weren't an experienced contact crew. We weren't Imperial scouts. We weren't even contract system surveyors. What we were was a bunch of college students on the equivalent of a joy ride. And now, here we were, on the verge of meeting extra-terrestrials. What were the protocols? Was what we were doing even *legal*, now that we knew the scope of it all? After all, we weren't sanctioned diplomats or anything.

On the other hand, I was technically a Lieutenant in the Navy. Maybe that would count for something.

Sure. At my court martial for incompetence.

"Are you OK, Kitra?" Marta's voice brought me back to myself.

I turned and raised my eyebrows in a shrug. "Feeling inadequate."

She smiled softly. "Me too. But we're the ones who are here. I bet the folks who stumbled on the Bugs and Pinky's people felt the same way." Marta added, "We're just looking around. The experts will be here eventually."

I took a deep breath and nodded. Go big, or go home, and there was no chance of going home. Not yet.

We walked past the statues to an arc of what seemed to be benches. They didn't tell me much — a bench is a bench — except that the beings who used them couldn't have been much bigger than human, if at all. Looking at the building beyond suggested the same. It was several stories tall, with seams at regular intervals that suggested floors, but it was strangely windowless. A lovely arched and covered promenade lined its front. All of it was of roughly human dimension. But as prettily as it was constructed, it had the same drab exterior as everything else in the square, a medium brown with tan patches interspersed, as if the paint were faded or coming off. No, that felt wrong. I examined the facade more closely.

The patches didn't seem to correspond with the more exposed surfaces. They were spread out more or less evenly. Decoration? They seemed too random for that. It was more like a characteristic of the building material, itself. I walked and ran my hand along a wall. It looked and felt unpainted. Maybe whomever built them liked the mottling. Or maybe they had a building Maker that only worked in raw material. I frowned. Would they even have Makers at this level of technology?

I stepped back. They might not have been picky about color, but they did have some kind of aesthetic sense. Above the gaping entrance there was a set of decorative ridges and bumps raised in a random pattern. It reminded me vaguely of the cursive in Fareedh's *Koran*, but more intricate.

I called out to Marta, "Is the signal inside?"

"Yeah. Definitely."

There was no help for it. We had to go in there. I suddenly felt very ill-prepared.

"Peter," I commed, "Why didn't we bring...how do you call

them…drones?"

Peter's voice rang in my ears, broadcast from his safe position inside the ship. "Why are you asking me?"

"You're the guy who builds stuff."

"What do I know about drones?" he protested. "Anyway, they're illegal."

"Only on Vatan," I pointed out.

"Well, pick one up next time you're on Hyvilma, then."

"You're a big help."

"Sorry."

Fareedh sauntered in front of me, hands in the pockets of his suit. "Well, if Grond the Foolhardy isn't here to lead the charge, why not let Lionel scout things out."

Pinky padded forward. "You're not going in there alone, pal."

I blew out a deep breath. "We'll explore it together. I don't want any of us separated from each other. Besides, what would anyone outside be standing guard against?"

We approached the jamb of the building's entrance. At first, I'd thought there was no door, but now I saw that the door was jammed open somehow. The edges of them, big rectangles from the look of things, stuck out about an inch from their slots. The light from outside quickly thinned, and there were no lights inside. I torched my *sayar* and shined it along the walls, the others following suit.

We were in a big room, maybe a foyer. Seats lined the walls, and there were sculptures in the corners. Our footsteps echoed hollowly on the tile or stone or whatever it was we were walking on. There was mottling on the walls in here, too, though it was less noticeable in the feeble natural light and in the ovals of our torchshine. There weren't any pictures or holo sprawls as decoration, but they might have just been turned off.

Dust motes danced in our beams as we walked toward what looked like a reception area, complete with a desk in front of a weirdly configured chair. I stared at it, trying to reconcile its shape with the statue outside. It seemed to fit.

I turned my attention to the desk. Physical objects lay strewn across it, more loose stuff than I was used to seeing in a work setting. A big rectangular pad spread darkly over half of it. That was the stand-out item, but there were also what looked like fuzzy balls and what must have been a coffee mug, or at least, a cup for maybe some kind of hot drink. It was a glazed shade of mud, but what it lacked in color, it made up for in texture. I ran my fingertips over the spiderweb design, smudging away a light layer of dust, before shining my torch inside. It was dry, of course, though the stains inside stood out brightly: deep purple. I set the thing down, starting a little at the overloud clunk it made.

"We go in?" Pinky asked, gesturing toward the hallway inside. It was completely dark.

Marta drummed her fingers nervously on the beamer at her hip. She was the only one of us who was armed. We'd left the other beamer back on the ship. They were the only weapons we had, and these only because we'd liberated them from the Puritans all those weeks ago. I suppose my new Lieutenant's commission the *Faucon's* captain had given me entitled me to some kind of sidearm, a stunner or a gummer maybe, but I hadn't asked for one.

I looked at Marta, and she nodded meaningfully to her *sayar*; the signal was coming from deeper in the building.

"We go in," I said, trudging forward.

The walls were reflective. The torchlight danced and scattered, filling the long corridor nicely and revealing a bunch of doors on both sides. Some were open, some were closed; all were on hinges. None of them slid or folded. The only auto-door was the opening to the building itself.

"My brother used to play this game with me," Fareedh said, his voice a little thin. "There was one big hall in our house, and at night, Iskender would hide inside one of the rooms off of it. He'd jump out with a yell and scare me half to death."

I turned to face him, annoyed. "Thanks for sharing," I said.

He shrugged. "Sorry. Just nervous."

Marta stepped forward, putting big hands on both our shoulders. "Leave it to Ukko," she said, trotting forward. She shined her torch into the two open doors ahead, left and right.

"Nobody in these," she said. "Surprise, surprise."

I joined her and peered into the rightward one. The main feature was four desks joined together to make a star, all flanked by those weird chairs. What does an alien office look like? I don't know, but that's what it felt like. Same with the room behind the leftward door.

Marta was already trotting ahead to the next set of entrances. These were closed, but they opened readily. She shrugged. "More of the same."

We went on like that for a bit, Marta leading the charge, and the rest of us following behind. That first floor was mostly offices, or some kind of work rooms. No beds or suchlike to suggest a residence or a hospital. One of the chambers was bigger than the other, with lots of chairs and small tables. A cafeteria? An auditorium? Again, the layer of dust, and the feeling of sudden abandonment. A couple of the chairs were on their sides, and there were a few items littering the floor. I took a closer look at one of them: a cup like the one I'd seen in the foyer.

"Where did they go?" Pinky asked no one in particular.

I opened my mouth to answer, but Marta's excited voice came over the suit comms, "Guys, come look at this."

We joined her in a rush. The room she was in was almost as big as the cafeteria, but it was completely different. A long oval table, sort of off-white, filled the middle, and the walls were lined with shelves from floor to ceiling. Marta had something in her hand, which she tossed to me. I squeaked, but managed to catch it.

It was a fist-sized ball, like the ones we'd seen on the foyer desk. I ran my fingertips over its fuzzy edges, the thin fabric of my suit muffling the sensation slightly. No, fuzzy wasn't the right word. Patterned. The surface wasn't made of fibers or hairs or anything, but a rigid, rubbery stuff. It yielded when I pressed, but then bounced right back, the pattern intact.

"These shelves are crammed with them," Marta said. I looked up and saw she was right. But they weren't strewn haphazardly. Each ball had its own little place, separated from its neighbor by a thin plastic wall. The shelves, themselves, though the same innocuous off-white as the table, weren't featureless. They were decorated with the same raised bumps and dashes we'd seen on the outside of the building. Inspecting them closer, it became clear that the pattern under each ball was slightly different, and there was a clear, slight separation beneath each pattern, linking them to the balls above them.

"I think these are labels," I said, excitedly. "This must be writing."

Fareedh strode over to my side, his gaze flickering intently from label to label. He ran his fingers across them.

"Braille," he said.

"You think?" Marta asked.

"Yeah. The patterns are three dimensional."

Pinky's baritone piped up, "Perhaps that's simply an artifact of the printing process. Or an aesthetic choice."

Fareedh shrugged bony shoulders. "Just a hunch."

Pinky ambled over to run his pseudofingers over the labels, too, his suit molding to accommodate his shifting shape. "I don't disagree. But the symbols we saw outside the building, if that was text, were raised, too, and only a giant could run its fingers over those."

"Well, either way," I said, setting my *sayar* to record holo, "if we get enough of this stuff, maybe the ship's *sayar* can decode it into French." My heart skipped a beat as my words sank in. This was real first contact stuff! If only there were someone here to actually contact.

"But what do you think these balls are?" Marta had one in each hand, and her eyes went from one to the other.

"Why don't you come back to the ship and find out," Peter's voice commed in our ears, a little urgently, I thought. "We can scan them and see what they're all about."

Fareedh's calm voice had a touch of reproach, "We can do that here, too." He had his *sayar* generate a a flat, featureless display of pinkish light. At his command, it drifted forward, passing through one of the balls. He called it back, sending it through the next ball over. I stopped my holo-ing to watch what he came up with.

"They're both of the same material," he said. "Some kind of hydrocarbon plastic. But look." He popped up a display big enough for us all to see with the balls side by side. "They're not identical. I mean, the pattern is unique on each of them." He pursed his lips to the side, the expression perfectly visible behind his bubble helmet. "Maybe these are data units. Like for a *sayar*."

I was dubious. "What do you mean?"

Fareedh chuckled in reply, "People used weird stuff to store data on in the early days. Tape, paper, even metal platters."

That didn't make any sense to me. In my mind, *sayar* information was glowy pieces of energy. It didn't exist physically anywhere. It just *was*. But talking about storage put me onto a train of thought. A way people used to bind information.

"Oh!" I exclaimed. "Maybe they're books." I'd never seen a physical book, but they were described in the novels I read on my *sayar*. From what I'd read, all the text was printed with special Makers onto pieces of paper pressed into rectangular prisms.

"Round, fuzzy books?" Fareedh retorted. "Plus, these grooves don't look anything like the labels."

Now it was my turn to shrug.

"Maybe they have different eyes for each type of writing? Maybe they've got print writing and…what do you call it…cursive?" It was dawning on me just how alien these people must be. I'd been thinking in terms of what I knew, but maybe that was wrong. Was this a library? A temple? And beyond physiology, if they were really a thousand years behind us in technology, that'd be its own set of differences. I started to feel in over my head. If only one of the aliens was here to explain themselves.

And then I remembered. There weren't any aliens around at all.

I put the ball back in its niche. I felt like a looter. Gone was any trace of the enthusiasm I'd felt before.

"There are a bunch of floors to this building," I said. "If the signal's not coming from this one, let's see if we can find a way to the others."

Marta looked nonplussed at my change of attitude, but she just nodded, putting her own balls back. Fareedh followed our example.

The end of the hall terminated in a couple of portals. One was a big, closed, set of metal double-doors. An anti-grav lift? No labels, and also no power. I waved my hands around, but nothing happened. So I tried the side door. It was gray and looked substantial. On it were dots, dashes, and curlicues taking up much of the portal's surface. That was unique. Why single this one out so much?

It opened; all I had to do was press against the clammy surface, and it swung back smoothly on some kind of pivot.

I directed my torchlight inside and quickly saw what the narrow chamber was for.

"Stairs," I called out. "They go up. Oh, and down, too." I hadn't expected a basement.

Fareedh grunted in response. Pinky asked, "Which way?"

I felt dizzy looking up the endless flight of stairs. The idea of hiking up them didn't sound appealing.

"Marta?" I asked.

She looked at her *sayar*. "It's coming from below."

"Whew."

I watched my step. There was no rail, and the aliens must have had longer legs than me.

The bottom of the steps ended in another door, labeled with raised scrawl just like the other. This one had a handle. I eyed it, the fingers of my right hand rubbing against each other nervously. Then I reached out to tug the portal open.

It jiggled but stayed put. It didn't seem locked, just jammed shut. I pulled harder. It moved maybe a couple of millimeters but no farther.

"May I?" Pinky's voice rang hollowly in the stairwell, flatly over my comms.

I stepped aside, and Pinky elbowed past me. He gripped at the handle, his paw-like hands growing and solidifying as I watched. His arms swelled, too. They didn't ripple or get definition like Peter's, but they looked powerful, nevertheless. Pinky leaned back, straining harder, without a sound.

Suddenly, the door flew open with a loud *pop*, as if the air inside had been at a different pressure. He angled back away from the door, but his three wide feet were stable, and he didn't tumble over. With a gracious bow, he waved a splayed hand toward the dark entrance, his arms already shrinking.

"Your Ladyship," he said smoothly, no pant to his breath.

I snorted silently and walked in, flickering my torch up to light the way.

At first, all I saw was the dancing dust. There was no illumination, but as I crossed the threshold, I thought I felt a strange tingling in my inner ears, a mild jangling in my nerves. Was I just scared? No, as I spun around, playing my light along the walls, it seemed directional, stronger when I faced away from the door than otherwise. It wasn't unpleasant, just odd, and somehow external.

Marta's voice echoed in the hard-walled room, maybe five meters on a side, "Hey, do you feel that?"

"Yeah," I said.

"What are you talking about?" Fareedh asked.

Pinky trotted in and said, "I *hear* it. Some kind of ultrasonics."

My torched *sayar* spotlit a bank of machinery lining a wall. It was complex and metallic, utterly incomprehensible; primitive-looking. "Coming from that?"

"No, not the ultrasonics," Pinky said, stepping up to the machines. "But I'll wager this is the source of the broadcast." He ran his stubby fingers over a kind of console. "This is a transmitter," he said.

There were no blinky lights or indicators to suggest it was even working, much less a comms device.

"How do you know?" I asked.

He turned and pointed meaningfully at his head-bump. That wasn't where his brain was, of course, but he was doing it for expression, not accuracy. "L' éclair," he said simply.

Fareedh caught his meaning. "You can tell a transmitter, even an alien one?"

"Sure. Those knobs probably control the frequency, and that rod-looking thing is probably a microphone."

Marta consulted her *sayar*. "You're right. This is it. Every time you talk, the signal jiggles."

Pinky inclined slightly and put his 'head' right up to the thin cylinder he'd pointed out. "Hello! This is your host, Pinky, speaking!"

Even as he was talking, I heard a shout of pain through my comms: Peter yelling, "Aaargh!"

"What's wrong?" Marta shouted.

"Ugh. Nothing," Peter said ruefully. "I'd just left the broadcast monitor on full gain. Pinky, you talk too loud."

"You *listen* too loud," Pinky replied. Turning to face us, he said, "Well, there you go."

I raised my hand to rub at my jaw, hit my helmet instead and lowered it sheepishly. "So they left their comms on, but didn't stick around to keep talking. Or put in an automatic message, if they even have recorded messages."

Fareedh was musing, "They can't have been gone too long. Otherwise the thing wouldn't be running, would it?"

Peter's voice came through again, "Depends on their battery technology. Or maybe they've got an emergency generator. Could be photovoltaic, though I don't see anything like that on the roof."

More and more, it was looking like the aliens had all just…left, and in a hurry. Why? And where to?

My eyes lit on another door against the back wall. Probably some kind of storage closet or something. Well, we were here. Might as well check it out before going back to the ship.

This was another hinged portal, and it, too, was stuck, but didn't seem locked. Pinky sidled up next to me, but I waved him away. The door didn't seem too badly jammed. One big tug did the job, and it was open. I pulled my torched *sayar* from my armpit where I'd tucked it and flashed the light inside.

It wasn't a storage closet. It was a vault. Filled with…

My eyes tried to parse the weird tableau. Long, irregular shapes covered in cloth lay heaped on the floor. There was no rhyme or reason to their placement. The fabric was colorless in the bright light of the *sayar*, like the scraps we'd seen outside, but what it covered was a mix of dark and light, flesh-toned browns and darker patches, some almost black.

Flesh-toned…

A scream echoed against the walls, piercing my ears. My scream, I realized.

Bodies. Dozens of bodies sprawled in hideous contortions. They were like that statue outside, the alien, but in all the colors of decay, all in twisted final agony. Their faces were blank and withered, like dried-up plastic bags.

I dimly felt hands grasping at me, and I jerked away, still screaming, my throat raw with it. My eyes locked on a roomful of death.

Now I was being dragged back into the first chamber. I struggled, my boot kicking something soft, and I heard a cry of pain amid the echoes of my cries. Restraints looped around my arms, binding them to my chest, and my voice cracked into silence, my breath now coming in ragged, heaving sobs.

"Kitra!" someone was shouting. "Kitra!" It was right next to me, and it sounded a million kilometers away.

"Close the damned door," someone else ordered. There was a

slam. Light beams danced crazily, then settled down. I didn't need the door open or the lights. I could still see them. Dead. All of them dead.

"Kitra, please," a deep voice said.

"W..wha..?"

"Kitra, it's me. You're safe. I won't let anything hurt you." The restraints around me tightened slightly in a pulse.

My gaze flickered down. I was girdled by something white, matte and smooth. I blinked away the blur of tears and recognized what I was looking at: suit fabric. It was Pinky. He'd grabbed me, pulled me out of there.

"What's going on down there?" Peter called out in a tight voice. "I can be out the airlock in five minutes."

Marta was kneeling in front of me, her gaze almost level with mine. "No, don't, Peter. We're alright." She searched my face, her eyes wide with concern. "Kitra, we're going to take you back to the ship, okay?"

My muscles were taut, poised to spring, to hurl me into some dark corner. By degrees, they loosened. I slumped into Pinky's grasp. I closed my eyes tight, then opened them. My heart was still racing. It felt like only Pinky's hug was keeping it inside my chest. But I was here again. I saw Fareedh and Marta and the transmitter and the closed door. A clear pane seemed to fall in my mind with an almost audible clang, a shield from what I'd just seen. I focused on Marta's face, her beautiful, worried features.

"I..." The words wouldn't come. My throat was a desert, a baked plain. I wanted to say I was okay. That I didn't need to be dragged back to the ship.

What I managed, finally, was a nod.

Chapter Five

Launch +40

The rest of the city was worse.

There weren't many corpses in the streets. All of the aliens had died months before, long enough for animals and decomposition and weather to take their toll.

But inside the buildings, they were endless: stinking ones crammed into vaults, and skeletal ones slumped in ones, twos, and threes over furniture in what had to be homes. Those latter were the ones who hadn't had access to shelters, though being in sealed vaults hadn't helped any of them. Whatever had killed them had worked quickly, infiltrated everywhere.

I learned all this second-hand. I felt like a coward, staying behind to guard the ship, but the others had insisted. I'd put on a brave face, insisted I was alright, but they knew.

I'm not good with dead things.

I come by it honestly. My father passed away when I was three. Some kind of defect in his brain: he just went to sleep and never woke up. I hadn't understood it at the time, and it didn't even really upset me much at the time. What do you know when you're three?

And then *L' Emmisaire* exploded when I was ten, taking mom away from me forever. At least during the times I was awake. She was still there in my dreams. Almost every night, I was back on the emissary ship, the alarms going off and the decks shuddering. These days, it wasn't just mom who was shoving me into the lifeboat, but dad, too, his dark features clearer than I could ever remember in waking.

Once, during the period after that when I wouldn't even go outside, my uncle suggested I get a pet. I screamed and threw something at him. Pets die faster than people, I knew.

Pinky had saved me then, coming to see me when I'd failed to make an appearance at school, hadn't returned his comms. He'd taken me in his pseudopods and made a circle for me, a place for us to be as close as two beings can be.

I shivered, recalling how close I'd come to losing Pinky just weeks ago. I don't know what I'd have done if he'd died at Hyvilma. I brooded on that a lot these days.

The solitude had given me one thing, at least: time to come up with a name for the world. I'd settled on Pesadumbre, the Spanish word for grief. No one had objected.

"We're coming back, Kitra," Peter's tired voice came over the comms, bringing me back to reality — sentinel duty on the bridge. I acknowledged the call and got up from my seat to greet them outside the airlock. On the way through the wardroom, I caught sight of Jub-Jub clacking its claws eagerly against the enclosure. Its food dish was full, but it clearly wanted something. I went over and it stretched out jointed arms, climbing up toward me.

"Okay, okay," I said, opening up the cage. Jub-Jub was out and in my arms in a flash. I would have fallen over if the table hadn't been behind me. Now the little thing was settling down, sprawled out on my chest. It wasn't going anywhere if it could help it.

I clutched it. Did Jub-Jub *know*? Like Pinky had known? I scritched at the creature's carapaced head, which it extended further in seeming contentment. It helped. The city, maybe the whole continent was dead, but we weren't. My friends weren't. The thought sustained me as I went aft.

Marta was the first out of the airlock. They were going one by one, taking the full several minutes of the sterilizing decontamination cycle. Marta's green suit crackled with static electricity as she enfolded me in a hug, Jub-Jub and all. The creature seemed completely unfazed.

"How're you doing?" she asked softly.

I stiffened. Marta sensed it and started to back away. "Sorry," she said. "I don't mean to mother you."

Instantly chagrined, I tightened my grip to keep her from going. "No, no, you're fine." Marta's solicitous attention had annoyed me when we were going out, been one of the reasons I'd broken things off. But I *was* fragile right now, and this was her love language. I needed to shed bad habits. "What did you find?" I asked.

She let her arms slide down, clasping my elbows gently. "The same. Plenty of unaffected fauna and flora. A half-year's worth of dust." She paused, her tongue between her teeth.

"And a city's worth of bodies," I finished for her. My mind clamped down hard on the image trying to materialize in it.

Marta nodded.

"Still no clue what did it?"

She let go entirely, folding her arms and pursing her lips before replying, "Lots of clues. All of them died where they fell. Whatever it was, it acted fast. That says nerve agent to me. But even with a human, I couldn't tell without an autopsy. With an alien, I'd have no way of knowing what 'normal' was for comparison."

The phrase 'nerve agent" made me uncomfortable. "You sure we aren't tracking this stuff into the ship?"

Marta shook her head, brown curls bobbing. "The sterilizer would break down anything on the outside of the suits, and if there were any leaks, we'd have found out way back on the way to the *Faucon*."

I smiled a little at that. Hard, orbital vacuum, like the kind we'd jumped through to sneak onto the embattled cruiser, has a way of letting you know if your suit isn't airtight.

"Anyway," Peter called from behind Marta, his heavy bootsteps thudding toward us, "Whatever it is, or was, is selective. If it doesn't hurt anything else on the planet, it's sure not going to bug us."

He came up, and Marta stepped aside. It looked like Peter was planning to hug me too — everyone was being extra touchy-feely lately — but then he saw Jub-Jub draped across my collarbones and stopped short, settling for a pat on my arm instead.

Peter turned to Marta. "Sweetie, I think we're done with this creepy city. That's four areas, all the same, and all we have to show for it is more of these." He pulled out one of the fuzzy balls, like the one we'd found in the library or whatever in that first building.

"Where did that one come from?" I asked.

"Some kind of stand by the side of an avenue," he said. "It had fallen over, probably from a storm, but there was a sealed box of these next to a bunch of others that had been scattered. My *sayar* said they were all identical, down to the individual grooves."

Marta nodded enthusiastically. "I've done a couple of scans. The grooves have repeating sequences. Well, sort of. They have short stretches that show up over and over again."

"Huh!" I grunted. "Like words? Handwriting?" I peered at the grooves. They didn't look like writing at all.

"Like something. I'd have to spend some time on them." She turned to Peter. "If we're done," she said, "what do we do now? Go home? Go somewhere else?"

I started to answer, but Pinky's voice came over the comms, "Wait for us!"

"Don't worry, gumdrop," Peter said, "We won't decide without you."

"Better not!"

The extra time gave me a chance to make coffee properly. I had to do something with my hands, and I wanted my brain clear if decisions were going to be made. I put Jub-Jub back in its enclosure, resolving to be fully pulled together by the time they were back.

I'd just turned off the heat so the coffee wouldn't boil and make the brew too bitter when Pinky came in. Then *he* gave me a hug too. But it never bothered me when he did.

"Fareedh's decontaminating now," Pinky said. Looking over at my metal *cezve* pot, he asked, "Did you make anything for me?"

"Coffee's not good enough for you?" Peter teased.

Pinky made a show of wrinkling up the crude features of his "head" in disgust. It had been a while since he'd mimicked human expressions, I realized. Lately, he'd stuck to changing colors, sometimes altering his scent slightly, which I'd assumed was more natural for him. I tried to remember the last time he'd made a face. Was it before or after his fusion with L' éclair?

"S'alright. I'll just see if the Maker will mix turpentine and cedar." He disengaged from me and began to work the machine. Now it was Peter's turn to make a face.

Thankfully, by the time Fareedh arrived, his hair unbound and rather tousled, Pinky had settled on a cocktail of flowery esters that didn't clash too badly with the smell of coffee. I got out the set of cups

I had inherited from my mother and filled them. There were only five, since one had shattered on our first flight. I hadn't used them while Sirena had been on board; I hadn't wanted anyone to feel left out. Now we sat, hands wrapped around our cups as if it were a cold day during Wind season.

Fareedh broke the silence first, "We should check out other cities. It's a big continent."

"I think it's a waste of time," Peter replied. Fareedh shot an uncharacteristically miffed look at Peter, and Peter quickly added, "I mean, if we're not getting active transmissions, we're probably not going to find anyone in the cities." He cleared his throat. "Maybe we should be looking in the wilderness, where someone could hide out from this stuff."

"Won't that be like finding a needle in a haystack?" I asked. "The nice thing about cities is that's where there's lots of people."

Pinky waved his three pseudo-hands palm out, "We don't have to do the whole continent. If we fly in a straight line from one side to the other at night, we could detect hot spots. If they're building fires, for instance."

"We'll miss so much," Marta objected. "And since the wildlife is untouched, telling a campsite from a herd of goats will be almost impossible."

"I just don't know that I can handle another city full of…another city like that one," Peter said. He was speaking for himself, but his eyes flickered up at me. I felt both grateful and embarrassed at the same time.

Quiet again. I took a sip of coffee, scalding. It left a spicy afterglow that braced me as much as the caffeine.

Deep breath. Then, "Marta, how many signals did you detect during our orbit?"

She gave me a little smile. "I'd have to check the log, but," her eyes unfocused as she thought, then snapped back into clarity, "…five. Two strong ones on this continent, three on the other. Some other faint ones that might have been broadcasts, or they might have been something natural. I didn't look too close."

"Okay," I said, leaning forward. The others followed suit, I noticed, except for Pinky, whose pink skin became a touch darker. "I agree with Marta. We're not going to find anyone through a random search, and anyway, we're not a survey team. I'm not comfortable roaming around on a wild planet, especially when we've only got so much in the way of supplies. If folks are alive in the country, they'll probably stay alive until we can get help. If they're not, well, there's no hurry anyway. I think we should stick to where there's power. At least there, we *know* there's a chance of life."

I put a hand on one of Pinky's arms. "We can go slow, do the infrared thing. Fuel's not an issue, not with all the water on this planet."

Peter said, "And when we get to another city, are we going to go through all that again?" He eyed me, gauging my reaction.

I licked my lips. "It doesn't have to be a comprehensive search. I think we'll know sooner rather than later. We should still try, though." I sounded braver than I felt. But Fareedh gave me a starburst of a smile, and that helped a lot.

"When do we leave?" Pinky asked.

I looked at my half-drained cup of coffee. "Well, I think sleep is out of the question for a little while, and it's..." I looked at the clock on the wall. It was done up analog style, programmed with 24-hour ship time and 27-hour time for the planet. Local sunset was only an hour away. "...almost night. Is everyone awake enough to be on their toes? We need to be ready to act fast if we get tracked by a missile radar again."

General rumble of agreement. Fareedh put an appreciative hand on Peter's shoulder, and the engineer's pale face flushed slightly. It was kind of adorable.

"Liftoff in sixty minutes, then," I said.

We could have made it to the other signal, at the other end of the continent, in less than an hour. But that would have meant a suborbital arc, rockets blasting, and you can't scan the ground like that. So I took us across the landmass on thrusters, trying to compromise between closeness to the surface for detection purposes and keeping enough altitude in case something shot at us.

Of course, the planet wasn't flat, which meant our flight path wasn't level. Seeing the ground wasn't a problem, at least, since it stood out well enough in infrared for maneuvering. Every so often, I switched the Window to the visual spectrum. Each time, I felt a little less hope. Like before, there weren't any dots of light. No constant streetlamps, no flickering fires. Infrared showed up things like rivers and lakes and the asphalt of empty cities just fine, but no sign of living people. Then the rumpled landscape became obscured with clouds, a storm front covering half the continent. I considered diving under the cloud deck, then quickly gave up the thought. That would put us too close to the ground, and anyway, what fires were we going to see in the rain?

I shifted in my seat and stretched. There's only so long caffeine and concern can keep you alert. I caught a glimpse of Fareedh knuckling his eyes, and soon after, I heard Peter's ostentatious yawn. Only Pinky seemed unaffected, but I knew he needed his version of sleep, too. I pumped up the thrust. If we couldn't see, we might as well make up the time.

About fifteen minutes later, Marta called out, "I'm getting the signal."

"Anything on it?" Peter and I asked at the same time.

"No. Unmodulated. Just a carrier wave."

We hovered over the spot at about 1,000 meters altitude. I looked "down" at the ground through one of the displays in the Window. It was dark in visual and mottled gray in infrared. I checked for water vapor to see if it was obscuring our view, but no, the clouds had cleared up on the way here. That was ground we were seeing: no lights, no heat from vehicles or people. I thought about flicking on the deep radar, then thought twice about it because of missile concerns. But what really decided me was that there was no point. There were probably buildings below, which would show up fine in deep radar, but it wouldn't show people. It was all just so futile. I didn't want to deal with another city of corpses, even if it felt like our obligation.

"Everything all right?" Pinky asked. He noticed my hesitation.

Instead of answering him, I called out, "Marta, you recorded all the signals we picked up in our first orbit, right?"

"Sure. That's automatic. Why?"

"Can you analyze them or run them through the ship's *sayar* or whatever? If one of them is sending a message, even an automated one, that seems like a better lead than chasing blanks."

I swiveled to see her reaction, since I didn't need to keep my eyes on the controls to hover. She shrugged, but smiled, a little wearily. "I didn't notice anything, first time out, but I'll go through them again. I'll check on the faint ones, too."

A quick glance at the fuel gauge showed us at 81%. I thought about topping off. On the other hand, setting up the tube was always a minor pain. On the Pinky hand, Peter'd be doing it…

I smiled a little at the image of Peter shouldering the flexible fueling pipe. The first time he'd set it up, to test it before our very first flight, he'd carried it over his head, showing off his strength. It was light at first, but halfway to the starport reservoir, the length of it had become too much for him, and he'd tripped and landed flat on his stomach, arms and legs splayed. He'd always used the cart after that.

I jerked as a strange warbling filled the air, like the cascade of a waterfall going up and down in pitch. A roar of static underlay it all, and just barely above that, I made out what sounded like an irregular stream of belches.

"What is *that*?" I cried out. Marta turned it down.

"*Napakymppi*," she said softly, but with not a little pride. "Modulated transmission. This is what it sounds like in the upper sideband." The waterfall muted and the rude noises became low tones. Meaningless, but they sounded artificial. "That was one of the faint ones. I had to run some filters before I could make anything out of it, but it's definitely sending."

Pinky's color had deepened, and he was gliding his paw over his console. I glanced at the new display he was poring over, a tangle of jagged lines that pulsed in time with the audible tones. "No repeats, either," Pinky said. "Probably not a recorded message."

Peter broke in, "It could be just, I dunno, weather telemetry or something."

"Using enough power to be picked up from orbit?" Pinky countered with a disbelieving tone.

"There's only one way to find out," I said. "Anyway, it's the most promising lead, and I honestly don't feel like checking out another dead city. At night."

"I agree," Marta said. I smiled gratefully at her.

"It's a few hours before dawn where we want to go," Pinky noted,

"And at least an hour to get there."

"Sleep," Fareedh said simply, making a show of crossing his arms and laying them on his panel, his head on top. A display popped up at the touch of his elbow: a shimmering graph half protruding from his spill of hair.

"All right," I said, stifling my own yawn. "Why don't we find someplace safe to park and get some sleep. Pinky, maybe some island without anybody on it?" I swallowed. "I mean, that never had people on it."

I felt a warm, rubbery pseudopod on my arm. "I know what you meant."

Seven hours later, we were hovering over the source of the broadcast. Another cityscape, rather different from the one we'd gotten so familiar with over the past week, filled the downward view. It was monochromatic, like the other city, but all the buildings were a pretty blue. And where the other city had been laid out in sweeping arcs, this one was a more traditional grid. Perhaps the other city had grown organically, and this one was more deliberately planned. No, that felt wrong. There had been an intentional quality to the other city, too, like its outlines had been aesthetically inspired, not randomly evolved.

"Hey, look at this!" Pinky called excitedly.

I sat up and set my coffee in the panel, its surface indenting to keep the mug upright.

Pinky went on, "Power output, infrared signatures, and...I think...movement. What does this look like to you?"

My eyes flicked from Pinky back to the ground view. The sun was just past local noon with respect to the ground so the shadows below were short, meaning less contrast for making out details. Then Pinky upped the magnification. Now we were looking at a single city street, and there was some kind of motion going on. Cars? No, too small. But there were definitely individual somethings moving up and down the avenue.

Fareedh was out of his chair, looking over our shoulders. "Could those be people?" he asked.

"We can find out, but we'll have to go lower," Pinky said.

"They might shoot at us," Peter noted.

"They haven't yet," Marta replied. There had been no ping of missile radars, either. Not once.

"I'd still rather not plop us down in the middle of them," I said, eyeing the blurry amblers. Their motion was slow, but steady. I reached for the display Pinky had put up, sliding the view sideways with a curl of my fingers until a flat square came into view. It wasn't a plaza like where we'd landed before, but more of a widened intersection of roads. I satisfied myself that there was nothing moving over it.

"Here," I decided. "We can set down and it's a short walk. If they charge us, we can take off again. Otherwise, we can go to them and see what they are."

It was easier said than done. As I took us down, I saw the square was smaller than I'd thought. I had to switch completely to manual to make sure I didn't scrape against the curbs, buildings, and other bumpy shapes that flanked the lanes. I wasn't worried about lighter debris. The force of the thrusters would scatter any light stuff that lay on the slate-gray pavement. I shuddered, thinking of what had littered the streets of the other city. Thankfully, I didn't see anything blow away in the downward-looking display.

At last, we were down. Fuel was at 71%. I'd opted for speed rather than efficiency on the way in, using thrusters the entire distance. I figured we'd attract a lot more missiles if we rode on a column of fire rather than using the quieter, invisible antigrav thrusters. In any event, we'd made it down safe. Slowly, I uncurled stiff fingers from the sticks and let out a breath. I swiveled to find Peter already out of his chair.

"You can stay if you want," he said, a little too casually.

Fifty corpses sprawled haphazardly like a forest of discarded deuterium tanks, all painted in a riot of decomposition. Blank faces glaring at me, reflecting the light of the torch in a flare of accusation.

I cleared my mind with a quick jerk of my head. "You're on sentinel duty," I said.

"Now look…"

I forced a smile. "You're the one I trust *Majera* with most."

"*Paska*," he snorted.

"What was that?"

Now he was smiling, warmly and unaffected. Something he'd picked up from Marta, maybe. "You heard me," he said. "But okay. I'll watch the house."

I got up, steeled myself, and moved to leave the bridge, but a strong hand gripped my arm. I turned to face him, and he wrapped me in an unexpected hug. A genuine one, not one of those half-hearted one-arm deals. And when he let go, his eyes were bright. He looked at me intently, his cheeks slightly flushed, and said, "Be careful."

I nodded, then smiled for real. "I will," I said softly. "Promise."

Marta and Fareedh insisted on going first, which was fine. That left Pinky to go out with me. I'd never suited up with him, which proved to be interesting. Pinky didn't need a helmet. He took his outfit from the wall, a shapeless thing like a deflated white raft, and suddenly it was a meter-and-a-half tall tent. He slithered inside, and the thing collapsed to become form fitting, a pane of clear material about a foot square showing pink Pinky skin. Two swirly eyespots swam into view. All he needed now was the oxygen tank.

"Where do I hook this up?" I asked helplessly. He was a featureless mound.

"On my back, of course."

"*Where* is your back?"

"Opposite my front."

My lips pressed together and I tapped his tank with my forefinger.

"Oh, where's your imagination?" Pinky asked with a sigh. He grew two arms and three legs over the course of about ten seconds, his eyespots becoming level with my chin. Then he turned around. Now there was a ridged circle right between his newly grown shoulders I was certain hadn't been there before. It fit the tank's outlet, and I checked to make sure there was no leakage. His suit was a nice piece of engineering.

He had less trouble getting the tank on me and making sure my helmet, once I'd sealed and bubbled it, was on tight.

"Allez-hop!" Pinky called, cycling the airlock.

Chapter Six

Alien air and sunlight poured in. It was brighter here, and according to my suit thermometer, warmer. Marta and Fareedh's heads both came into view simultaneously from either side of the door, their bubble helmets giving them faint halos. The sight made a giggle snort wetly through my nose, and I felt my cheeks color as I sniffled back the snot. I waved, my voice coming out a little shaky: "Is it…like the other place?"

Fareedh shook his head. "Come check it out."

Pinky sidled out next to me and made a fair likeness of a human whistle. It was obvious why.

"It's clean," I exclaimed.

Despite what the view had shown as we landed, I'd still half-expected what we'd seen before on the other continent: trash, shreds of cloth, maybe remains of beings. Instead, the flat space looked almost polished, its huge square slabs reflecting the noon light like burnished aluminum. Maybe the reflected heat was why it was so warm. No, the temperature made sense for the latitude the city was on, and my suit readouts said the tiles were actually cooler than the air. A neat trick. The aliens were an interesting mix of advanced and primitive.

"There's no way this is natural," Marta was saying. "Someone is sweeping the streets." She had a hopeful glow in her eyes, and she took my hand and squeezed. My smile reflected her excitement, and fingers entwined, we headed down the street toward the movement we'd spotted from above.

"Just be careful, guys," Peter's voice rang in our ears.

Pinky ran nimbly to Fareedh's side. "Yes. Hold me, Fareedh. Keep me safe."

"Of course, beloved," he said, taking one of Pinky's paws in his long, delicate fingers. Was he teasing me? My ears burned a bit, but Marta gripped my hand more tightly, keeping me from letting go.

Pinky jokes aside, Peter was right. We were in unknown territory, and we couldn't just traipse in. I steered the gang to the walls lining one side of the street. The architecture was squat, brutal even, but the walls were intricately textured when you looked closely: a sort of pixelated mosaic cunningly set into the bright blue walls. There was none of the splotchiness that characterized the city on the other continent. Instead, there were gentle swirls in the walls, like currents frozen in the building material. Pretty, I thought, beneath a thick layer of apprehension.

Hugging the sides of the building, we approached the corner of the lane we'd seen the movement on. Before we reached it, Pinky raced in front of me, holding me back with his posterior arm.

"Let me," he said, extending and narrowing his head. He snaked his eyespots around the corner at the tip of a thin tentacle. After a moment, he simply exclaimed, "Wow…"

Curiosity moved me. I peeked around Pinky's white-suited bulk.

It was like a robot convention.

Big boxy ones on wheels. Little lozenge-shaped ones with skirts covering where they touched the ground. Robots with spindly arms. One bulky one that clanked on treads like an asteroid rover. While I watched, a gust of wind blew a spray of trash or leaves from far down the street, two squat buildings hulking on either side of the lane. No sooner had the breeze-blown stuff hit the ground than three of the small cruisers and one of the big machines with arms trundled after it. A flurry of activity later, the street was clean, and the robots involved disappeared into a small portal in the building whose wall we were pressed against.

I'd seen robots before. They aren't uncommon on human worlds, though labor laws and tradition have kept them rare on Vatan. But I'd never seen a gathering like this. Part of it was the sheer numbers, but what really stood out was how obviously archaic they were. The robots I'd seen were smooth, streamlined things, emphasizing form as well as function. Sometimes they looked a bit like people, other times like mobile works of art, but always there was a perfected sleekness.

These guys were unpainted, metal-and-plastic machines that looked more like something Peter might have prototyped for a class than mass-produced devices. Yet mass-produced they must have been, because there were too many, too many alike in form, for them to be a series of test one-offs.

It was mesmerizing, all of these mechanical creatures. Could they be intelligent? Were these the aliens who were broadcasting? Were there two races on the planet, one biological, one robotic?

"Take me to your leader," Pinky said quietly.

"I was thinking the same thing," I answered.

Marta's hand squeezed mine. "What's going on?" She was still behind me and couldn't see.

Pinky said, "Hold on. I have an idea." With hardly a ripple in his suit, Pinky's shape began to change. He elongated, and his legs took on a triple-jointed look, hips high up on his slendering frame.

"You're going to pretend to be an alien?" I whispered. "What if it doesn't work?"

He shrugged, unable to express himself with colors. "The suit is supposed to be beam-proof."

With that, he walked out around the corner.

Fareedh lurched out after him. "What the…?" I grabbed his bony hips before he could plunge out into the open. He looked wide-eyed at me, then surveyed the street. He didn't relax, exactly, but he stopped trying to follow Pinky.

One of the boxy ones, silver and cream and big as a mini-car, rolled up toward Pinky. I held my breath. The robot opened up a door in its frame and extended a little ramp to the ground. It *was* a mini-car! Pinky made a show of looking at it, curled paws on his hips. Then he gave it a jaunty wave and carried on down the street. None of the other machines gave him so much as a second look.

Could we follow Pinky? Did we look enough like the aliens to fool the robots? There was only one way to find out. I slipped out of Marta's grasp, pressed past Fareedh, and stepped out onto the street, ready to dart back on a moment's notice.

No reaction. Okay then.

I let my breath out in a relieved sigh and waved the others to follow me. Fareedh joined me, then Marta, her hand twitching over her beamer.

"I don't think these are the aliens," I said, walking by the mechanicals.

"No," Fareedh agreed. "Pretty primitive, I'd say."

"Yeah," Marta said. "No anti-grav or even air hover. And they're just sitting or going on set paths."

"But why *here*?" I wondered aloud.

Fareedh fingered his *sayar*. "Well, I could try hacking into one of them."

"Wait, you can do that?" Marta asked, her tone a bit awed.

He waggled his eyebrows at Pinky, whose "face" behind the suit's viewpane flushed salmon with amusement.

"He's not serious," I guessed.

"I'm not serious," Fareedh agreed. "It's hard enough accessing a foreign *sayar*, let alone an *alien* one."

"Oh," Marta said, sounding more relieved than disappointed. "Yeah, I didn't think so." Marta was a programmer, too.

My smile faded as quickly as it had been born. Clowning around didn't seem appropriate right now, for every reason. "Well, regardless of why they're here," I said, "this seems to be the spot they want to be at. Let's see what's got them so interested." I pointed at the obvious entrance. It was a wide, square, double doorway perched about a meter off the ground at the end of a stone ramp. Like all the other buildings here, and in the other city, for that matter, there were no windows visible, making the edifice look unsettling, like a jail.

I turned toward the door…and paused. I wanted to move, but the image of the shelter in the other city froze me in my tracks. I stared hard at the doors, and my mind started to flash images of what might lie behind. The sound of the rolling, whirring and clunking robots was a continuous low din on the street, but in my imagination, it was all deathly still.

A grip on my shoulder made me jump. One of *them*…no, just Pinky.

"You can stay out here if you need to," he said. "One of us can keep you company."

I shook my head. "No, I'm alright," I lied. "Besides, either way, we'll be fine. Either there will be live people, or they won't be alive, and they won't be able to hurt us."

I shivered at the words, but my feet were moving again, up the ramp and under the ornate portico, the one concession to aesthetics the designers had made. No, that wasn't quite true. There was filigree on and around the door jamb. It had just looked like texture from the street. I ran a gloved finger over the intricate grooves in the door. It reminded me somehow of the fuzzy balls we'd collected on the other continent.

Then, with a confidence I didn't feel, I shoved at the door. It opened with only the slightest resistance, rotating inward. Just like the other building, it was dark inside, the light from the street illuminating just a narrow path. I torched my *sayar* and held it in front of me, looking to either side as I walked in.

The room was huge, some sort of foyer, with tall, square pillars at intervals. Whether they held up the roof or were just decorative, I couldn't tell. Movement caught my eye, and I shined light on it. A little lozenge robot chittered to itself as it rolled in a slow spiral along the floor. A cleaning robot? I looked down. The floor was tiled in a subtle checkerboard pattern. I knelt down and ran my fingers over it. It wasn't painted, but there was a texture to it. And no dust whatsoever.

Fareedh unfolded a set of light displays hovering above his *sayar*. Instead of a directional torch, they acted like a portable lamp, better for local illumination than our narrow beams. He darted over to a sort of kiosk in the middle. It was a splash of mottled mustard amidst the pale blue of the distant walls. I went closer and saw that its texture was random and blotchy, like the walls of the buildings in the other city.

"Think fast," Fareedh said, and there was something in my hands before I'd even realized I'd reached out to catch it. A fuzzy cube with the same grooving as on the balls in the other city's cafeteria/library. I ran my thumb over the ridges and thought. "Pinky, back on the ship, you said there was power, right?"

"Yep." He had ambled up beside me.

"Well, where is it?"

Pinky played with his *sayar* using two hands, growing a little third arm and fingers to hold the cube. "It's right here, lots of it. The building is powered."

"Then why are the lights out?" I asked.

Marta piped up, "What lights?" She pointed her torched *sayar* upwards, casting a bright oval of light that far outshone the glow from Fareedh's displays. "The ceiling is smooth."

"We have smooth ceiling lights," I pointed out.

"Sure," she said, "but it doesn't fit with the tech level. And that looks like naked concrete, or whatever they're using. Not some kind of panel."

Fareedh ran his hand over the smooth kiosk material, a contemplative look on his face. "Maybe they don't need light."

"How do they *see*?" I asked.

He shrugged. "Maybe they don't." He looked over at Marta. "You're the biologist."

"I'll withhold judgment. Besides, there may be someone here to ask." She smiled hopefully, though it looked a bit strained.

"Maybe this little guy?" Pinky asked, pointing at something on the flat desk or table inside the kiosk. Several somethings. He picked them up and handed one apiece to each of us, starting with Marta.

"It's a doll!" she exclaimed.

Sure enough, they looked like the statue we'd seen on the other continent, and like Pinky did now: an alien in miniature. They were all in a kind of muddy greenish plastic. The proportions on mine weren't quite the same. Thicker around the middle, with shorter arms and legs. They matched the dimensions of some of the smaller bodies we'd found in the other city. Marta had tentatively identified them as juveniles.

"Mine's a blockhead," Fareedh observed.

"That's not a nice thing to say," Pinky rejoined.

"No, I mean a literal blockhead."

"Mine, too," Marta said.

I set the cube Fareedh had given me down on the desk and examined my doll more closely, quickly spotting the issue. The doll was pretty detailed, with the joints intricately carved or lasered, but the cubical head looked almost like a parody of the rounded alien heads we'd seen.

"Why would a receptionist have a set of dolls on its desk?"

Pinky shrugged. "I like dolls. No one says you have to grow out of them."

"Yeah, but you grow…" Fareedh started.

He never got to finish. A screeching noise from farther inside the building set my teeth on edge. Four torch beams, including my own, sprang up in unison, spotlighting a portal in the far wall, a rectangular blackness that gave no clue as to what lay beyond. As quickly as it had started, the sound was gone. I looked at the others. Fareedh's face was pale in the dim glow of his neck ring lights, and Marta's eyes were wide. The piercing sound tore through the near-quiet again, like something in agony. Every goosebump on my body stood at attention.

"Someone's hurt?" Pinky wondered.

"Something's going on," Fareedh added. "Do we," he paused, "see what it is?"

Marta dropped her doll to the floor with a clatter and clutched her beamer tightly with both hands, torched *sayar* pressed against the weapon to shine where it was pointing. She looked at me for an answer.

I had to clear my throat, and then my "yes" was cut off by another peal from the dark portal, so I simply nodded and tucked my doll in one of my suit pockets.

Marta insisted on taking the lead, padding with grace despite her size toward the far wall. I stole a look over my shoulder before joining her. The light streaming in from outside looked so far away now.

We reached the portal, and it opened on a hallway running not farther in, but paralleling the wall. There was an open door ahead, and more down both directions of the corridor. Then I squeaked as a swift wave of my torched *sayar* returned glinting reflections in the passageway. Two more robots: blocky, meter-high machines that bristled with strange projections. I froze. I meant to jump back to the safety of the portal, but my feet wouldn't move. Then I saw that the robots were stock-still and completely silent. I took a ginger step toward them, and they didn't so much as twitch. I let out a breath. Maybe they were burned out. Or deactivated.

My relief lasted approximately three seconds. Then there was another screech, this time with a curiously cut off ending. This time, the direction was clear, and we dashed down the hallway to the right, sidestepping around the dead mechanicals. A different sound came down the hall now, of clattering impacts. We followed the noise, through a couple of turns, past an enlargement of the corridor that wasn't precisely a room, ending at a closed door. A strange hum emanated from within, rising and falling in volume.

"Hello?" I called out, crouched next to the door. All I got back was more humming. I hadn't really expected an answer.

It was Pinky who moved first, running his left hand over the door until he found something like a handle or knob. The door swung in on hinges, and it was dark as space inside, too. Again, Marta elbowed Pinky aside to take the lead, beamer out in front of her. I appreciated her wanting to keep us safe, but I worried about how leading with a gun might look to whomever we found inside.

The room seemed to be for storage. At least, that's what the rows of skeletal shelves suggested, and whatever was on them reflected my torch light metallically. There was a thud, and the humming stopped, followed by that same screech, deafening now. I tried to put the heels of my palms to my ears, but I only managed to bump them against my helmet instead.

Fareedh, instead of flinching from the sound, headed toward it, disappearing behind a rack. The sound got louder, and I frantically turned on the noise-canceling function on the suit. Now the screech was muted, distorted into a kind of musical static, and I could think again.

The sound abruptly stopped, and I heard Fareedh's "a-ha!" faintly in my ears. I cautiously took off the sound filter as we rounded the corner of the rack, and there was our lanky friend holding up a cubical robot, a meter wide, by one corner. The thing looked like a twin of the dead robots we'd passed in the corridor. This one was quite alive, however, jerking slightly, back and forth, trying to roll on little casters at each corner. The end Fareedh was holding up was discolored, and there were bits of equipment scattered all around the robot. The shelves around it were bare, as if the machine had knocked them down.

"Its wheel's off," Fareedh explained. "The poor guy was stuck, scraping against the floor."

I didn't think the robot looked very sympathetic. Squat and rugged, it struggled against Fareedh's grip. It had a kind of head mounted on top, cubical, with an eye-like detector. Pinky went around the other side and helped Fareedh hold the robot in place. The head swiveled, keeping him in his sights the entire time. There was a weird flutter in my ears. At the same time, my *sayar* popped up a little warning display. The robot was throwing off some kind of waves, low energy, in the subsonic band.

"It's very interested in you," Marta said, her voice tight.

"I can tell," Pinky said. "It tickles, whatever it's doing."

I laughed, a little nervously. Then there was a loud bang and a bright flash that left me stunned and dazzled. I jumped back, smacking against one of the shelves, and the whole thing started to give way. I tumbled onto my back, an enormous clatter registering dully against my ringing ears. Another flash and shot, then another. I thought I heard Fareedh call out. His voice was staticky. Then Marta was between me and the robot, the beamer in her outstretched hand. I watched over my knees in a daze as she fired, and the robot's head exploded in a shower of sparks.

"What's going on?" I heard Peter comm.

"The thing shot at Pinky," Fareedh's voice shouted from far away.

I struggled to get up, disentangling myself from the toppled shelves. "Are you okay?" I cried. My ears rang a high whine now. I couldn't see a thing, but my *sayar*, still torched, lay near the dented corner of the now-dead robot. I picked it up and shined it around the room.

Pinky was gone!

Then something like the dying wheeze of a synthetic calliope called out from behind the shelves that were still standing. "Over here," it said.

We all scrambled around the shelf toward the voice. Pressed up against the wall, something that looked like a giant white beach ball shivered. It took me a moment to recognize my oldest friend, but the suit's view pane was unmistakable, as were the two swirly eyespots behind it. They glistened in our torchglow.

"Okay, now I can't see, either," he managed.

We quickly lowered our *sayars*. Marta got to him first, feeling for holes in his suit. Lord, I couldn't take it if he was seriously hurt again. "Where'd you get hit, Pinky?" I asked.

"Right here in this room. Didn't you see?"

I could have throttled him. But his voice already sounded stronger. The healing power of comedy.

"Seriously, Pinky. What happened?"

He quivered. "Projectile weapon, I think. That *hurt*, but the suit's designed for impacts, too. The shot got spread out evenly across my body." He let out a long, terrific exhale, which got perceptibly louder as my ears recovered. Legs, arms, and head bump began emerging from the spherical form until he was close to his original shape. "I think I'm alright, but I don't want to do that again. I'm already going to be one big bruise tonight."

Peter's shout came through loud and clear. "Get back to the ship *now*."

"You don't have to tell us twice," Fareedh answered. He went to the door, then turned to see if we were following.

That pause saved his life. A flash lit the hallway behind him, followed by the sound of something hard hitting a wall. Fareedh ducked back inside.

"They're shooting at us," he said dazedly.

"Who?" I demanded.

He shook his head. "All I saw was the flash. Maybe it's more robots."

"Why would they get hostile all of a sudden?" I barked. It didn't make any sense.

"Maybe I made them mad when I lifted their pal," Fareedh rattled off.

Pinky said, "But he shot at *me*," pointing to the robot Marta had shot.

"Well, *that* one shot at *me!*" Fareedh said, jerking a thumb down the corridor.

The sound of wheels on tile grew louder.

"Guys," I said nervously. "They're coming closer."

Fareedh shook his head. "I'm not going out there again."

"Ambush," Marta called. "Quick. Behind the shelves."

It was a better idea than staying out in plain sight. We followed her lead, pressing ourselves against the far wall, then blinking out our torched *sayars* and neck lights. My eyes adjusted to the dark as the sound of the robots' whirs grew louder. It dawned on me that the complex was not entirely lightless. Through the alien parts lined haphazardly on the racks, I could just make out the door: a slightly lighter patch of dark against the complete dark of the storage room wall. It wasn't coming from the building's lobby; that was too far away. I was still wondering about it when a loud clank came from the door. A robot was here.

I felt rather than saw Marta's arms go up, beamer pointed at the door. She had a perfect shot.

More clanking and a whir as the robot crossed the door's threshold and found traction inside the storage room.

"Shoot," I hissed. What was she waiting for?

Nothing. Then, "I can't." Her voice had a strange quaver.

"Do you need a light?" I went to torch my *sayar* again.

"No!" she squealed, and her arm brushed wildly against my head. The motion knocked something off the shelf, and there was a flash and boom. Marta cried out, and something clattered against the floor, sparks flying. It was the beamer, I realized dimly. Now Marta was crouched, unarmed. I felt her shuddering. *I* was shuddering.

Peter's worried voice came through the comms. "Guys, what's happening now?"

More whirring. The robot was having trouble navigating the mess its dead sibling had made, both before and after we'd gotten here, but it was trying its best to close the distance.

"We've got to get out of here," Fareedh said. His voice was low, emotionless.

"Marta lost the gun," I whispered. "She may be hurt."

"I'm not hurt," she said quickly, her voice trembling. I clung to her, as much for my comfort as hers. We were plain targets unless we did something.

"Maybe we can blind it with the *sayars*," I blurted.

"It doesn't have any trouble with its own flashes," Fareedh snapped back.

As if in agreement, there was another shot and a deafening ricochet. I had no clue what it was shooting at. I prayed no one had been hit.

The sound of the robot echoed against the walls. Its casters had found purchase on the floor. It was coming after us. And we were defenseless.

"I have an idea," Pinky said. "Wish me luck."

My nerves prickled with ice. I grabbed Marta and prepared to jump. If Pinky was making a distraction, we had to be ready to move.

There was a rustle as Pinky began to pad out of our hiding place. The lights around his suit's view pane sprang softly to light, illuminating his blockish lump of a head.

I stiffened, then paused. What was the point? Even if we somehow got to the door, we couldn't leave Pinky behind. In any event, there were probably more sentry robots out there. And Pinky couldn't count on his suit holding out against more shots.

Then I was blinking at the realization that I'd had time to thinks all of those thoughts.

The robot wasn't shooting.

Pinky's head was a glowing willow-o'-the-wisp, bobbing forward, eclipsed and then visible through the items on the shelves. He walked forward slowly but deliberately. It was too dark to see what the robot was doing, and I dared not torch my *sayar*. But still, no shot rang out. Finally, Pinky was practically on top of the murderous machine, and I saw it dimly reflected in the suit's glow. Not only was the sentinel not shooting, it wasn't even looking at Pinky anymore. Its head swiveled back and forth, and then it jerked to life again, rolling back and out of sight. The sound of its casters dwindled, then disappeared.

I let my breath out in a gust, then clutched at Marta. I risked turning my neck lights on; I had to know if she'd been hit. Marta was looking at me, or rather, she seemed to be looking through me, her face strangely blank, slack.

"Marta..." I began.

At the sound of my voice her expression animated, and her eyes focused. Then she jumped as Fareedh placed his hand on her shoulder.

"Are you alright?" he asked.

Marta swallowed, then nodded weakly. Fareedh slumped with relief, his hands gripping her tightly.

But Peter was blind to all of this. His comm came through, mad with worry. "Sweetie, are you okay?"

I saw Fareedh smile, his teeth a gleam in my suit glow. "I'm fine, honey."

"*Dammit!*" Peter growled.

"We got shot at," I said. "We're not being shot at now." I looked for Pinky and spotted him easily. He'd just torched his *sayar* again, and he seemed to be waiting patiently by the door.

"Why isn't Marta answering?" the voice over the comms demanded.

Marta had to clear her throat. "I'm fine." She shook her head, hard. I watched with worry as she got to her feet. She switched her bubble lights on again and took a deep breath. The uncertainty left her posture. She looked like Marta again, strong and solid.

"Sorry about that," she added, her voice firm, if a little thin. I could feel my smile in response flickering. Fareedh slowly released her.

Pinky hailed us from the door. "I think we're clear."

"What if we run into more of those guys?" I shot back. I remembered those silent robots we'd passed in the halls. Obviously, they hadn't been dead. Just waiting for an alarm.

"I'll lead the way. But I don't think it'll be a problem."

He sounded a lot more confident than the situation warranted, but he *had* managed to quiet that robot. Did Pinky have some kind of weird psychic powers I didn't know about? I got up and brushed myself off. No, there was no such thing as psionics.

Right?

Pinky was again the spitting image of the alien we saw in the other city, with overlong arms and two legs. He was slender around the waist; he'd put most of his mass into his limbs and stretched out for maximum height. I filed in behind him, my view of the corridor almost completely obscured. Fareedh followed with Marta bringing up the rear. If we got shot at from the front, Pinky could probably protect us. I didn't like the idea of him being a shield, but his confident pace kept me from arguing.

I jumped as a little cleaning robot rolled past me, nonchalant of our presence. It got past Fareedh, but Marta dodged the wrong way, and they collided. I held my breath, ready to tackle the thing if I had to, but it just turned 90 degrees, trundled to the hall wall, then went back to its original heading, disappearing into the dark. There weren't any sentry robots. Where had they gone?

Now we were at the doorway to the lobby. The place was still quietly abuzz with robots, but now each whirr and clank pulled at my frayed nerves. A shot could come out of nowhere, and that'd be that.

"Here's the real test," Fareedh said, his voice subdued. "Peter, tell Iskender I died a coward."

"I'm going to kill you when you get back."

"I love you, too."

Pinky turned and gripped my gloved hands in his alien paws. "I'll go first," he said. "Don't worry. Nothing's going to shoot at me."

"They'd better not," I said as strongly as I could manage. "I'll rip them apart if they do."

There was no expression in his face, of course, and his color was just a washed out pink in the glow of his suit, but he gave my hands a little squeeze before letting go. Then he turned back around and walked through the door without so much as a bracing breath.

One second. Two seconds. Three.

"Come on out, guys. We're all friends here," he boomed.

I stepped slowly out into the lobby, still expecting a shot at any moment. The open door to the outside was a bright rectangle far ahead. Pinky stood silhouetted in the streaming light, waving his thin arms encouragingly. Dimly, I saw at least two of those guard bots, maybe the ones we'd seen in the hall. They rolled right up to him and then past without pause or a second look. He even gave them a jaunty salute as he strode forward. Talk about *chutzpah*!

I made sure Fareedh and Marta were behind me. They were, Marta looking tense, Fareedh wearing a bemused half smile. In no time, we were past the kiosk, at the door, out on the street. Pinky led us past the robot convention at a brisk pace, but not a run, and we rounded the corner without a single one of the mechanicals even seeming to notice.

Once we were around the corner, the street seemed to heave under my feet, and I had to stop and brace myself against a wall. A loud exhale, Marta's I think, told me I wasn't the only one just this side of fainting. Fareedh steadied Marta, and Pinky came to my aid, his embrace awkward in his new shape.

With a half-hysterical chuckle, Fareedh wheezed, "How the hell did you manage that, Pinky?"

Keeping one hand gripped on my shoulder, he turned to Fareedh, pointed up at himself, and said, "I used my head."

"Wha…" He looked confused. But Marta was already exclaiming, "Oooh."

Pinky nodded. "She gets it."

"Gets what?" I demanded.

Marta gave Fareedh a little smile of thanks and let go of him. Then she dug out one of the dolls we'd gotten from the kiosk.

"The head. It's square," she said.

Right. Like Pinky. He didn't look quite as he had when we'd gone into the building. Now, his head was decidedly angular, not round. And the robots no longer had seen him as a threat. That could only mean one thing.

"The guys on the other continent, they aren't the same as the ones here," I said.

Marta nodded. "And they're the enemy."

"At least to the folks here," Pinky said. "It must have given that robot a turn to see what it thought was a bad guy infiltrating the Ministry of Defense, or Ahmed's Auto Parts, or wherever it was we were."

"But why didn't they shoot at you when we came in?" Fareedh asked.

Pinky shrugged. "The ones we passed weren't active, I guess. The one you found must have called in his friends. Maybe that was the pulse I felt, or maybe that was him registering me as an enemy shape." He wriggled, his harsh-planed head rippling a little. "It doesn't matter right now. Let's get back to the ship. I *hate* this hard-cornered shape."

I could believe it. It must have taken a lot of energy for Pinky to keep that sculptured form for so long. But as we hurried our way back toward *Majera*, it wasn't him I was really worried about. I took Marta's hand, and she gripped it like she was afraid of falling, all the way back to the ship.

Chapter Seven

Marta said hardly a word after we came back to the *Majera*. I tried giving her a hug in the wardroom. She didn't push away, but she wasn't really there, either. And she glared when Peter offered comfort, something I'd never seen her do before. It scared me.

First thing's first. I wanted us far from the city and its killer robots. Maybe they didn't see us as a threat anymore. Maybe they weren't going to bother us in that square. But the streets had been clean, which meant that, at some point, we would encounter them again. I didn't want to take any chances.

I lofted *Majera* and headed out from the city center, the robotic bustle quickly giving way to empty streets. And then…not so empty streets. Nausea clawed its way upward from my stomach, burning my chest.

I hovered several hundred meters up, refusing to get any closer to the ground. Even the blurry view from that height was enough. Here and there, bodies lay strewn in clumps. They were about human in size, roughly like the statues and dolls in form. Their ragged outlines lay contorted — by wind, animals, or in their final throes, who knew. Then I hit the thrusters to get away from that awful sight.

A couple dozen or so kilometers away, the last of the neighborhoods was just a hazy line on the horizon. I set us down on a wide plain. This way we'd have plenty of warning if anything came toward us.

I hugged myself. Nothing was going to come toward us. This continent was dead, too.

I wanted comfort. I wanted Marta. I shook my head to clear away the vision of the city and its dead. Marta needed help. Focus on that.

Maybe she wasn't in the mood for company, but I had to reach out, at least.

"Marta?" I commed, using voice, once I'd gotten to my stateroom.

She answered almost immediately. "I'm here."

"You want to talk? In my cabin, I mean. Just us."

"Yes," she said. No hesitation.

Marta didn't say anything. She just sort of stared glassily at the holo of Helmi Kader on the wall, the one with her standing over the ancient ruins she'd discovered on Talvi. Marta had once been jealous of my obsession with the archaeologist. Now, I couldn't read her expression at all. For all I could tell, she wasn't even seeing the holo.

"Um," I began. "Scratch your back?" It was the only thing I could think of.

She nodded, looking down at me as if noticing my existence for the first time. I bit my lip, returning the gaze silently. Eventually, she figured out what I was waiting for. She's always been too tall for me to take off her top without her crouching. With the ghost of a smile, she peeled the shirt she'd been wearing under her suit over her head and tossed it to the floor carelessly.

That also wasn't like her.

Marta lay herself silently on the bed, and I began to trail my short fingernails over her shoulders. She always enjoyed this more than backrubs, when she could convince me to do it. I was never sure I was doing it right, though she'd never complained. I wasn't sure, now. Soft as she was, I could still feel her stiffness, her muscles ridged and restless under her smooth skin. But after endless quiet minutes, she finally started to relax, her breath easing into a deeper, slower rhythm.

My mind was a kaleidoscope, fractured into shards of parallel thoughts. Was Marta going to be okay? Why had she frozen? Why were there robots on this continent and not the other? And would we have to make a grisly tour of more cities to confirm that they were all dead?

Marta broke the silence with a muffled, "I'm sorry."

I cleared my dry throat, reverie dashed. "For what?"

"Letting you down. Letting everyone down."

Tears misted my vision, and I bent forward to kiss her spine. "You didn't..." I began.

She went on as if I hadn't spoken. "Pinky was shot. Fareedh could have been shot. The robot could have shot *you*."

"It didn't. We're all fine," I stressed.

Now Marta was shaking, and when I brushed her hair aside to see her face, my fingers brushed tears.

"Hey..." I had no idea what to do. Our roles were reversed; I'd never had to comfort Marta, certainly not after something like this. I didn't know what was wrong or even how to ask. So I just lay there with her, my fingertips making what I hoped were soothing patterns along her back. I was prepared to do that as long as I had to—forever, even. A knot formed in my chest. It hurt so much to see my strong Marta like this.

Marta's sobs eventually subsided, but her eyes stayed open, shining, fixed on nothing. Finally, she said, "You're not asking me what happened."

"I wasn't going to push."

She was quiet for another stretch. Then she took a deep breath, and when she spoke, it was with calm tones, a little tight around the edges. "I just couldn't do it," she said. "It wasn't like I saw the robots as people or I had flashbacks to the *Faucon* or anything like that. My finger simply wouldn't push the firing stud."

"But you were able to blow up the first robot, the one that shot at Pinky."

Marta nodded. "Yeah. I did that without thinking. And then I felt sick. This weird chill just...enveloped me, head to toe, and it was all I could do not to throw up in the suit." Her voice went thin and rapid, "Then the next robot was coming, and you were all in danger, and I *couldn't do anything*." She pounded a fist into the mattress. "What's *wrong* with me, Kitra? I *like* guns."

A wild thought went through my head. Did the robots have some kind of fear ray that immobilized enemies? I put my arms around her, pressing my cheek between her soft shoulders. "Hey, you did fine. We made it out."

She rolled over abruptly, and before I knew it, she was pulling me close, my cheek to her sternum. I heard her heart pounding and her ragged intake of breath against my ear.

"I've been dreading this ever since Hyvilma, Kitra. Worrying that if I was ever in a fight again, I would freeze. So I just sort of shoved it all down. I figured it would work itself out over time."

My palms were against her sides, and I clutched her like she might fly away at any moment. "Hyvilma was hard." It was all I could think to say.

"You didn't kill anyone."

Stung, I whispered, "I'm sorry." Of course. How could I pretend to know what she was dealing with? She didn't need me. She needed therapy.

She tilted my head up, looking at me levelly. A crease furrowed her forehead. "I mean that's *good*. I didn't want you to have to. You shouldn't have to."

"I'm not a fragile flower," I said with irritation. "You don't have to protect me." I hated it when Marta mothered me. It was smothering.

"Yes I *do*," she went on vehemently. "I'm supposed to take care of you, to make sure you don't have to go through this. To make sure you don't lose anyone else you love." She added, with a sob, "What good am I if I can't do that?"

My resentment evaporated as quickly as it had appeared.

"What *good*?" I asked incredulously. "Good Lord, Marta. I wouldn't be here without you. I couldn't. If you hadn't signed up back home, we'd never have gotten off the ground. We couldn't have saved the Émilie. Rescued Fareedh's brother."

"But..." she began to interrupt.

"But more than that..." I persisted, my tone softening with a deep realization, "I *love* you. Lord, I love you more than anything. Let me protect *you* for a change."

Her eyes bored into mine, flicking side to side, searching. Then her breath came out in a slow gust, and a smile emerged under the shining eyes. "Okay." She sniffed and brushed her palm across her tears. "Okay," she repeated more firmly. "We can trade off." Her hands found mine and squeezed. Hard.

My grin faltered, then broadened, like a fire catching. How had I gone so long not understanding what had been driving Marta? Well, it didn't matter. I knew there was more to say, more to work out. I couldn't fix everything. But at least...at least I could help. Even just a little bit.

We sat there for I don't know how long, our fingers intertwined, both of us looking at each other. It was nice to be together like this, alive and feeling. All the death, the oppressive emptiness of the alien world, for the moment, it felt safely contained beyond the walls of the ship, warded off by what Marta and I were sharing. For just a little while, I forgot where we were, what surrounded us.

There was only so long we could just sit there. After a while, our faces reached a critical point of dopey. Marta let out a little snort, then looked surprised, like one of Pinky's fart noises had come out of her mouth.

That set me off. I don't have grace to my laughter, just donkey whinnies, right from the belly. Soon, Marta was ringing out high-pitched peals to match. We just couldn't stop. I looked away, tried to regain composure, but then I'd look back at her, and she'd make a face, and we'd be in fits again. Tears streamed down her pink cheeks, but now they were happy ones, and my vision blurred to match. She looked so silly, so beautiful.

We managed to stop, but only by studiously avoiding eye contact. We clung to each other, occasional hiccoughs shuddering us. With a happy grin, I rested my head on her broad chest. She was so warm.

And soft. And she smelled good.

I felt my tongue slide along the inside of my lips, and I shifted my weight. Now I felt warm. Well, more than warm. I reached for her hands again, ran my fingers over them. She made a contented sound, and I responded in kind, making a kind of harmony.

She gripped my hands suddenly, disengaged, and exclaimed, "Oh!" as if in revelation.

I looked up, nonplussed. She was staring at the wall, brows knit in thought. Then she looked at me and broke into a grin. "I think that's it!"

"Um. Okay. What's it?"

She laughed and shook her head, curls jiggling. "Sorry. I just Peter-ed there. The books. I think I know how to read them."

I blinked. "The books…you mean the alien ball things."

"Yes! Well, I have an idea."

I looked down at the floor, then back up into her eyes.

"And that's what you want to do right now?"

I must have sounded disappointed.

She took my fingers into hers again, blushed prettily, and said, "I'm not *just* like Peter. I can prioritize," she said, and leaned in for a kiss.

It was nice. Very nice…but we were both back in the wardroom twenty minutes later. So much for prioritizing! Still, it had been a good twenty minutes. More importantly, she wasn't upset anymore. At least, she didn't seem to be.

Fareedh and Peter weren't answering my text comms. Maybe they were asleep. Then I wondered if they were in the same room. I flushed a little at the thought. As much as it all made perfect sense, it was still a little hard to believe. And maybe I was a little jealous. No, not jealous, exactly. Maybe 'wistful' was the right word. Fareedh was a good guy, and it's not that I *wasn't* attracted to him. It's just that he had asked me out at a bad time. Turning him down had been the right choice then.

Of course, maybe being with him wasn't entirely off the table. After all, Marta didn't mind sharing Peter with him…

I shook my head. This was all new to me. When I looked up again, Pinky was there, looking comfortably stable on three legs. If we'd woken him up, he didn't seem resentful or the worse for wear.

"What's going on?" he asked, his holo-star voice as smooth as ever.

Marta grinned brightly and held out one of the grooved orbs. But before she could open her mouth to speak, Pinky took the ball with a "thanks" and promptly tucked it against his skin and consumed it.

I yelped. Marta exclaimed, "What are you doing?!"

Pinky's skin shifted from its normal pink to a muted orange, and he made gagging noises. Then, with an exaggerated 'ptui', he produced the ball from…from somewhere, and offered it back. "Tastes *terrible*," he said. "Why did you give me this?"

"Pinky," I managed, "don't hand that to me. It's got your guts all over it."

"Does *not*," he protested. "Look."

I expected it to be dripping with slime. It was perfectly dry. I looked back at him, and he was now flushed a deep salmon of amusement, quivering like jelly candy as if with laughter.

"But that thing was inside you!" Marta said.

"A ha!" was Pinky's reply. "At no time was the ball inside my body. Observe."

His color still bright, Pinky held the ball over his head with one three-fingered hand. "As you can see, there is nothing up my sleeve."

It was true—he wasn't wearing anything. As usual.

"Now. Watch."

Once again the artifact disappeared in a blur of motion. This time, though, I caught how he did it. As he pulled the ball to his middle, at the same time, he brought up his other oversized paw and also bulged out his middle. He then stood still, arms at his side, waiting expectantly.

I tapped at the other hand, the one that appeared never to have held the ball. Sure enough, he opened it and there it was, resting on his palm.

Marta clapped her hands. "That's really good, actually!"

Pinky bowed. "I've been practicing." Now he was tinted rose, as if he were blushing.

"That was terrific," I agreed grudgingly. I took the ball back and handed it to Marta. Then I coughed and prompted her, "You were saying?"

"Um, oh right," she said, taking back the ball. "So, I think I have an idea what these grooves are."

"It's where the flavor is," Pinky offered.

"Maybe," Marta said, straightfaced, "But they're something else, too." She smiled coyly. "You should have figured it out before me, now that you're back-up Comms Officer."

At that, Pinky cocked his stumpy "head" and turned a deep shade of peach. It was a new tint for him. Was he channeling his L'Eclair memories?

All at once, he regained his pink composure and snapped two of his pseudofingers. Sort of. They rubbed past each other with a dull thud. He gave it a few more attempts, succeeding on the third try with a creditable pop. "Thank you for your patience," he said.

"You got it?" Marta asked, looking pleased.

Pinky pulsed purple. "I think so. Sound waves?"

Marta bobbed her head vigorously. "Exactly."

"How did you figure it out?" he asked.

"Pots!" she said, as if it explained everything.

I was confused. "Um. These are pots?" They didn't look like pots.

"No. Hmmm. Have you ever turned a pot, Kitra?" Marta asked.

"Have I ever…you mean, upside down?"

"I guess not. When you turn a pot, or I guess *make* a pot, you're putting clay on a spinning wheel and shaping a bunch of successive layers. Sometimes you decorate it by running a stylus over the clay while it's still wet." She rotated the ball in her hand, tracing a tinted fingernail along its surface. "You get grooves that look a little like this."

"Okay," I said, still not getting it. Except, something was pinging inside my head. Something familiar. "Oh! I remember now. Arch 102. Ms. Kaya's class." Marta had taken it with me, which was awfully nice given that we hadn't even been going out anymore by that time.

Now it was Pinky's turn to be confused. "I've never made a pot nor taken an archaeology class. What are you talking about?"

Marta and I both started talking at the same time, but I quickly yielded the floor to her. "So, ancient pots with grooves," she explained. "It used to be that people thought that the stylus got jiggled, just a little, by the ambient sounds in the room as the grooves were being made. The thinking was that if you had a sophisticated enough *sayar*, you could extrapolate what sounds were happening while the pot was being turned. Maybe even the voice of the person making the pot."

"Yeah," I said. I turned to Marta, now confused. "The problem is, it doesn't work."

"No?" Pinky asked.

"Yeah," I said again. "Lots of things can make a stylus jiggle. Shaky hands. A wobbly table."

"Right," Marta said. "You can't *accidentally* put sound recordings into a physical medium."

Pinky said after a pause, "But you can put them in deliberately,"

"Right. I think that's what these are," Marta said brightly. "I think these are sound recordings. Like what we thought the pottery grooves would tell us." She peered at Pinky. "How did *you* figure it out?"

"Oh, you said it had to do with communications, so I just naturally thought of waves. Light waves. Sound waves." His pink deepened. "It's exciting, though, the idea of analog recordings on physical objects. I wonder if humans had something like this, back in the pre-spaceflight days."

I smiled at Pinky. "When did you get interested in human history?"

"History is important. It's what makes us," he said blandly. "And I *am* a communications officer." He crinkled his face, the eyespots narrowing for a moment. "Er. That is, I am now."

"Fair enough," I said, giving him a fond squeeze on the arm. I turned to Marta. "If the ball was marked on purpose, how would we get the sound out of it?"

"I'll just run it through the ship's *sayar*. We'll have to make some assumptions. I don't know if we'll get the relative pitch or volume right, but we might get something that could be translated."

"What made you think of this…you know, when you did?" I bit my lip and flushed a little, not quite able to look at Marta, but I had to know.

Marta shrugged. "Life's not a holodrama. Not everything has a trigger." She grinned sheepishly. "Okay, maybe there was. We made those funny little sounds, and I guess it brought back a memory."

I glanced at Pinky, a little embarrassed, but he just returned the gaze, eyespots sliding back and forth between us, without expression.

"Well, what are we waiting for?" he asked. "Let's figure out what's on these things."

Chapter Eight

It looked like it was going to be easy. Marta quickly put together a program that would read the grooves and translate them into sounds. As Marta began scanning the ball with a laser tool synched up to her *sayar*, Jub-Jub clacked its claws and watched through the pane of its enclosure, as if in anticipation.

"I'm making a 3D map," she explained. "This way, we won't have to use a beam every time we want to read the thing. We can just store it in the ship's *sayar* and manipulate the grooves how we want." Her eyes suddenly met mine. "Kitra, do you still have that cube that Fareedh tossed you?"

I blinked, trying to remember if I'd clipped it to my belt. Chagrined, I shook my head. "No, I left it there."

Peter and Fareedh were here now, too, the former just in shorts and the latter wearing a rainbow *dishdashah*. The hem of the skirt bottom barely went below his scrawny knees. He hadn't managed to bring back a cube either.

"That's OK," Marta said with a shrug. "We have plenty to work with."

"I wonder how the aliens read these things," Fareedh mused, sitting down at the table. "They were just out in the open, and we didn't find anything you'd stick them into."

Peter replied, "Maybe they all carried around some kind of tool. It's not like we carefully searched their bod..." His eyes flickered uneasily over to me. He coughed and finished, "searched them."

Marta finished and took the ball from the table to place it on a shelf. She expanded a display over the table with an enlarged holo of the same artifact. Her eyes narrowed as she pondered the image for a bit. Then she shrugged and picked a groove near the top. "Have to start somewhere," she said. "Might as well be here."

A moment later, sound came from the air, presumably reproduced by the ship's *sayar*. It was a clear tone, like a flute but flatter, warbling up and down in pitch. Sometimes it seemed to trill like a lazy bird call. Other times, it rose and fell smoothly. The volume changed subtly, too. This went on for a good five minutes, and then it stopped. By then, we'd all taken seats at the table. I was resting my chin in my hand, only half-listening by the end.

"What does that tell us?" I asked.

Marta frowned. "Nothing."

"It sounded like something," Peter said.

Pinky replied, "There's not enough information in what we heard. If it were a voice recording, there would be a lot more intricacy. More subtle variations." He drummed the table with three sausage-sized pseudofingers. "That was also really short, too. Is that the whole ball?"

Marta said, "Oh no. That was one ring."

"Wait," Pinky said, tinging peach again. "It's not a continuous groove? I thought it would all be one serial recording."

She shook her head. "No, all of the groove rings are separate. I did run the playback pretty slow, though."

Fareedh offered, "Maybe it's a collection of songs."

"Not very interesting ones," Peter said.

I suppressed a yawn. "Why don't we try one of the middle grooves, one of the long ones." I added, "And speed it up some. Otherwise, we'll be here all night."

"I'll do it at 4x," she said. "But I don't want to miss anything."

Fareedh shrugged. "Anything we don't hear with our ears, the ship's *sayar* can pick up. And it can run through it as many times as you like."

"Yeah, I suppose that's true," she said, her tone sheepish. "I just really want to hear what the aliens sound like."

That made sense. She was a biologist. She liked to know how life worked. Alien life most of all. Heck, she'd been insufferable around Pinky when she'd first met him until I asked her to back off. She hadn't been invasive—she wasn't X-raying him with her *sayar* or anything— just nosy. Pinky had been a good sport about it, but I could tell he'd been uncomfortable. He'd been very private about himself and his kind back then, only opening up recently. To her, and to the rest of us.

I also desperately wanted to hear the aliens, though for different reasons. Since we'd landed on this world, there had been nothing but the silence and the death. It shrouded us, muffling everything. If their voices really were captured on these balls, if I could hear them, it would be a kind of life amidst this worldwide grave. I craved that life, even if it was just a fossil.

Marta touched a groove near the ball's "equator" and let the program run again. This time, the warbles were bright and quick, but still in the same range of pitches. Marta must have adjusted for that so the squeals wouldn't go ultrasonic when sped up. I looked over at Pinky. His eyespots were drifting slowly apart and wandering. It was a bit unsettling, but I figured he was just concentrating on the sounds he was hearing, not concerned about his appearance. Marta, too, had an abstracted expression, focused on the sounds.

Fareedh nodded, as if he had satisfied himself of something. I looked the question at him, but he simply murmured, "there's more here." I tried to listen more intently, but I'm not a musician, and my ears are nothing special. Maybe the tone sounded a little fuzzier than the last time, but more or less, it seemed like the same thing.

Peter looked bored.

This went on for, I don't know, perhaps three minutes, this endless, meaningless electronic chirping. All of a sudden, the quality changed. Instead of clear, trilling tones, it was more like a long burst of static. Static with staccato undertones beneath the noise on top. Marta sat bolt upright at that, her face intent in concentration. Fareedh leaned forward, listening.

All at once, it was over, and we were back to the bird calls.

"Run that again," Fareedh said.

Marta was already doing it. We were back to the old speed, and when the static came on, I could hear the punctuated nature of it a lot better.

"That's digital data," Fareedh said. "I'd stake my guitar on it."

The harsh static was now a hail of individual raindrops, and underneath, I heard what sounded like a honking train alternating with the crash of waves, both with a sort of ragged texture. Like if I could listen more closely, or if Marta slowed the playback down further, I'd hear silence between the individual noises. It was eerie in a way I couldn't describe. It might have sounded familiar to Fareedh, but it was incomprehensibly alien to me.

When that section was done, Marta stopped the playback. She and Fareedh sat back with simultaneous exhales. They exchanged a grin.

"Can we read it?" Peter said. He was interested now.

"Which part?" Marta asked.

"I was thinking the digital part, but I guess the whole thing, if those *cui cuis* are translatable."

Pinky quivered. "Perhaps the analog portions *are* speech, but rendered in an artificial manner, which would strip them of their undertones."

I asked, "Like if a *sayar* were reproducing a voice, but without, I dunno, emotion?"

"More as if the aliens can somehow visualize the wave forms of their words, the sound patterns of their speech, and make a written text using stylized pictures of those wave forms."

Peter's eyebrows went up. "That's pretty wild."

"Well, it's a fun idea, if nothing else," Pinky said.

Fareedh offered, "I guess we can have the ship's *sayar* go over all the rings and all the patterns and see if it gets enough similar matches to put something together. Without a Rosetta Stone, though, I'm not sure how we'll know what any of it means."

I had an idea. "There were those labels on the shelves, and also the signs in front of the buildings. We could make some guesses from those."

Marta smiled at me, nodding as if her star pupil had given the right answer. It was the kind of thing that used to annoy me. It made me feel really good now. "That's a great idea." But then she quirked her lips to the side. "That still doesn't explain the static, or why the two rings were so different from each other." She rapped the table once with the fingers of both hands. "Oh, you're right, Fareedh. We can't listen to each one. I'll let the ship's *sayar* do some analysis. See how the grooves differ from each other, find common patterns, and take a crack at the digital stuff. What time is it anyway?"

All of us looked up at the wardroom clock, except for Peter, who went for his *sayar*. We were still on local time, so the days were longer. The sun had just set, but according to the ship's clock, it was already bedtime. I wasn't sleepy though.

"All-nighter?" I suggested.

Marta laughed. "This might take me a while. There's not much you can do to help. It's a one-person job."

Pinky raised a hand with an oversized finger. "Four player match of *Topatlatıcı*?"

"No fair," Marta pouted.

"We couldn't play with five, anyway," I pointed out. My fingers already twitched in anticipation. It had been a while since we'd played. *Topatlatıcı* had been a favorite hologame of ours before Fareedh had joined the group, sort of a virtual, two versus two football.

"Alright," she conceded. "But make some coffee and Majera Specials first?" She fluttered eyelashes over wide eyes.

I laughed. "Deal."

Launch +41

Pinky and I were zooming down the green and white checkerboard, passing the ball between us as we approached the pink goal. Peter's rotofoil, a single-person hovercraft, flew into view. I knew it was his because of the fuzzy *mortilki* that emblazoned it, goofy big eyes and all, which was his avatar in almost every game he played. The *mortilki* was Denizli's city mascot, one of the few native Vatan species that had been preserved since colonization, and Peter loved that thing. Peter's S&S character, Grond the Barbarian, wielded a Space Shield with a *mortiliki* on it, too.

Now that purple beast was staring at me, the fields of Peter's rotofoil clashing with mine, arresting my progress. I couldn't pass the ball, or it would get stuck in his field, and he'd have possession. We struggled at each other, Peter's taunts filling my ears.

Out of nowhere, Pinky's craft, spherical as ours were wedge-shaped, slammed into the flank of Peter's rotofoil. I cheered, but then I saw that the collision had jarred the ball loose. It flew straight toward Fareedh's rainbow-striped ship, now vectoring toward us at full speed. I began to call out to Pinky, then yelped as a giant human hand swung into view, palm out and waving.

Instinctively, I pulled my head back, out of the holo display my *sayar* had put up over the wardroom table. No longer immersed in the image, it flattened into two dimensions. I looked up to see Marta standing over me, wearing a tired but triumphant smile.

"Guys, I got something!" she cried.

"Gooooaaal!" Fareedh called out. An electronic victory tune sang out in concert with his announcement.

"No fair!" Pinky said, disengaging from his floating holo. "External interference."

Peter and Fareedh collapsed their displays, their grinning heads popping into existence. "All's fair in love and hovercraft," Peter said.

Marta made a face at him. "I didn't do it on purpose. Just for that, I'm teaming up with Kitra against you next time."

"Bring it on," Peter said, the smile not leaving his face.

Fareedh waggled his eyebrows suggestively, looking from Marta to Peter and then back again. Then, more soberly, he asked, "What did you get?"

An uncertain look clouded her features. "Well, I may be premature. But I've got *something*."

Pinky winked out his display and looked at Marta fixedly. "Something is better than..." and he launched into a perfect mimicry of the cacophony of strange sounds we'd heard earlier.

She took a deep breath. "Okay. Well, firstly, look at this." She waved her hand, and an image of the ball appeared, floating above the wardroom table. My *Topatlatıcı* display half-blocked it, and on the game screen, I could see Peter and Fareedh's goal drifting into view. For a moment, I had the mad temptation to pick up the ball and blast it through to score, now that the others had left the field. Instead, I crunched the display into the table with the palm of my hand, and it fizzled out of sight with a small flurry of sparks.

The artifact had been enhanced in holo. It rotated slowly, and a circle bisected it vertically, like a world's prime meridian.

"It's symmetrical. The grooves are the same on both sides. Maybe so you can read it from any direction," she said.

"Did you find words?" Peter asked.

"Well... that's the thing," she said. "Look."

The ball seemed to unroll like a spool of spaghetti into a stream of squiggly white lines, hundreds of them, in vertical rows. They made a virtual page extending across the table, a glowing wire fence through which I dimly saw Peter and Fareedh's faces.

Marta went on, "The *sayar* found a lot of vaguely close matches, but nothing it could fix consistently as words." A few short batches of squiggles began glowing more brightly in yellow. "These are the matches. You can see there aren't many."

Fareedh leaned forward, hand cradling his stubbly chin, and peered at the lines.

"Is it just me," he said, "or are some of the lines simpler than the others?"

Marta nodded. "You noticed that, too, huh? Yeah. They seem to be in batches."

I squinted at the lines until I saw what they were talking about, and then it was impossible to miss. They were in bands, five or six lines wide. The bottom ones in the bands had frenetic peaks and valleys separated by short, relatively flat bits. As I looked up the bands, I saw the lines became less complex until the top one in each was mostly smooth humps and dips.

Then Fareedh's eyes flashed, and a bright grin spread across his face. "Music!"

"Come again?" Peter asked.

Fareedh's lips quirked inward, as if he were stifling a reflexive response. Peter clearly got the message and dug an elbow into Fareedh's side.

"Ow! I didn't say anything. Anyway, look. It's like sheet music. You don't read it line by line. You read it simultaneously."

Marta clapped a hand to her soft cheek. "Why didn't I think of that?"

Fareedh preened. "You're not a musician..."

Pinky seemed to bounce in his chair. "Can we play a band instead of a line?"

Marta nodded. "Sure. I'll have to account for the distortion since they're not all quite the same length, being mapped to a sphere. Hang on a sec."

At the far right of the "sheet" of lines, a pink glow appeared, encompassing one of the bands. It began to drift slowly to the left, and instead of the chorus of bird calls I'd expected, there was a deep wheeze, scintillating with bright sounds. They rose and fell like before, with chirps and trills and slower variations, but this time, there was a depth. I frowned in concentration. It was like...like skin diving off the Denizli coast in summer, when the imported whales and sprawlerfishes were out in force. Those mournful calls combined with the rush of water past the ears.

A cold shiver prickled through me, the hairs on my arms standing on end, and I felt tears stinging, as the memory of the bleak and dead city, corpses like toppled trees, swelled and burst behind my now closed eyelids. I'd suppressed the thought for so long, but now the enormity of it all hit me. They were gone. All of them gone. This was all that was left.

The sound went on, a lone, raspy flute with a shadowy echo, for I don't know how long. Then it was done, or Marta turned it off. I opened my eyes. No one had said a word, and mine were not the only eyes that were wet. Even Pinky was affected; I recognized that subtle greenish tinge of sadness.

Fareedh broke the silence, clearing his throat. "How did you know which side to start from?"

"A guess," Marta answered. "The wave forms aren't symmetrical. When people speak, there's a sharper start and a tailing off at the end, so I looked for that."

She wiped her cheeks and inspected her *sayar*. Her eyes widened a little. "Look at this," she said.

There was a dramatic *ping* and the holographic sheet suddenly blossomed into a mosaic of rainbow colors. The lines were the same, but where there had been sporadic yellow glows to indicate possible words, now practically all of the bands were split up into bright sections, color-coded in various gradations. The legend 'MATCHES FOUND' floated on top.

"Sweet Infinity," Peter breathed.

Fareedh shifted in his chair. "We've got a vocabulary," he said. "Now we need a dictionary."

"What about the labels and the buildings?" I asked, remembering the earlier suggestion.

Fareedh thought, then clicked his tongue against his teeth in a negative. "I doubt that'll work. Those were single lines."

Pinky said, "Well, I still like the idea that their script is just a simplified version of their spoken wave forms. Those labels might have been even simpler forms."

"We can at least try," Marta said. She began fiddling with her *sayar* displays, occasionally muttering commands. I kept quiet. After a minute or two, some of the glowing "words" were encircled in vivid lavender.

"A ha!" Pinky crowed in triumph.

"It's just a few, though," Fareedh countered.

"Still, a ha!" Pinky wasn't ready to concede defeat.

I pored over the lines again. I felt like the weakest link, and I wanted to contribute somehow. Sounds weren't my thing, but color…

"Hey Marta," I began. "What's that purply sound?"

She pointed, "You mean this lavender here?"

"No. The short, darker ones." There seemed more of them than the other colors, and they always followed a gray stretch of flat quiet.

Marta played the sound in question. It was a high, double trill. Quite brief.

"Dunno," she said. "Maybe a kind of punctuation."

"*Before* a sentence?" Peter asked.

"Sirena's written language is like that," I noted.

"Huh."

If he was going to say anything else, it was drowned out by a loud growl, from his midsection. He didn't even look embarrassed, simply shrugging and saying, "I think it's time for breakfast."

"Lord," I said. "Did we really play that long?"

"Different days mess you up," Pinky reminded.

"So much for circadian rhythms," Marta said with a rueful smile.

Fareedh made to stand up. "Shall I put something together? Then we can hit the sack."

Peter joined him, heading toward the galley end of the wardroom. Marta sat down, pondering her *sayar* displays. "This still doesn't explain the digital bits."

"Oh yeah," I said. "I'd forgotten about those."

Fareedh called over his shoulder, "Does it help now that you're looking at bands instead of lines?"

Marta frowned. "Not really. If I superimpose them all like I did with the analog parts, I just get more dots. And anyway, with the digital stretches, the lines don't get simpler as you go toward the top. They're all the same complexity."

Pinky folded two sets of fingers together and placed them under his eyespots, mimicking a human pose of consideration. "All right, let's think about this." After a pause, he grew another arm from his chest and placed a third hand under the other two. When he was sure we'd noticed, he went on, "We didn't find any reader devices, so the balls were probably meant to be read with whatever the aliens use… or used, I guess…to see."

"It's weird," I said. "I liked your idea that the lines were sound waves turned into stylized script, but now that we've heard the playback done right, they sound like straight sound recordings. What could read something like that on sight?"

Pinky shrugged with all three arms. "Maybe they aren't seeing things at all. Maybe they use touch, or they have echo-location or something."

"We never did find any eyes on the...on them," Marta observed.

Peter turned around. As his body went sideways, the smell of what he was cooking wafted past his thick body. Sauteing onions. My mouth watered.

"If they're not using readers, then they'd have to be able to render those digital parts on sight. Or with whatever sense they were using. There's got to be some kind of standard protocol, some kind of format. The question is, what are those digital patches for?"

"Some kind of identification code?" I suggested. "Like they use on products in stores?"

"Or a Maker's mark," Marta said.

"Say..." Pinky's tone made us all look at him. "I think you're onto something," he went on. "The analog parts are words. Maybe the digital parts are something abstract. Images. Pictures."

"They don't look like pictures," Marta said.

"We just don't know the right way to look at them."

This sounded familiar, something else from one of my Archaeology classes. Digital pictures and aliens. I ran fingers through my hair, then winced. Yuck. It was dry and gross. I needed a shower. I surreptitiously sniffed under an arm. Okay, I was safe there, at least. Alright. Back to the topic at hand. Something about receiving images from extraterrestrials. No! *Sending* them.

"I got it!" I exclaimed. Thank you, Helmi Kader and puppy love, or I might never have taken those courses.

I saw that everyone was paying attention, even Fareedh, looking over his shoulder with a batter-covered finger in his mouth.

"It's like those messages sent out to the stars before Jump was invented. They'd beam a digital message that, if you decoded it right, would show things like stick-figure people and a map of the solar system and chemical formulas and stuff. They did it again on..." I searched my brain, "Gyula. One of the first Midworlds. Hold on. I've got a holo saved."

I went through my *sayar* and searched. It was one of my favorite images, and I found it quickly. I floated a display of the massive orbiting transmitter: a constellation of parabolic dishes, sparkling in sunlight against the blackness of space, forming the outline of a huge, circular structure.

"Do you have an example of one of the messages?" Marta asked hopefully.

"Yeah, I'm sure there's one in my textbooks."

She beamed at me. "Wonderful! I'll see what I can do with that."

Fareedh set a plate in front of Marta with a soft thud. An omelet steamed next to a crepe. They looked terrific.

"First," Fareedh said. "You're going to eat. And then maybe sleep."

"But I'm not tired…" she tried to say, but a yawn interrupted her. "Okay. Maybe a little nap."

Peter sidled up to her on the other side, putting a hand on her shoulder. "It'll keep," he said gently. "We can spare a few hours." *They're all gone. A few hours, a few weeks, a few years, what's the difference?* was the somber, unspoken subtext.

Marta nodded, taking a bite of egg. She didn't look convinced. And somehow, neither was I.

Chapter Nine

The tweet, tweet of my *sayar* slung me out of a deep sleep, banishing the images of a dream before they could crystallize into permanent memories. Marta calling. No, I realized, as the floating display came into focus. A general comm from Marta's *sayar*. The others were already on the call.

I looked over myself. I hadn't bothered to get dressed after the shower, and for a moment, I thought about just answering the comm that way. After all, Marta and I were going out, Fareedh had seen me like this once—if only by accident—and Pinky wouldn't care.

After a moment's consideration, I decided to wrap the sheet around me. Marta and I might be a thing, and she might be connected to Peter and Fareedh's thing, but *I* wasn't in on that thing. Was I even invited? Did I want to be?

I shook my head. The *sayar* was still tweeting at me, and there were more important issues at hand.

"What's up?" I said, my voice a lot raspier than I'd expected. I cleared my throat.

Four faces popped up, each in their own display. They were all in separate rooms. No, wait. Pinky was in Fareedh's. I could tell because Pinky's walls were featureless, whereas Fareedh's had that beautiful *mandala* tapestry.

"It's becoming cliché to say," Marta started, "but I've got something." She had dark circles under her eyes, and it was clear she hadn't slept much, counter to Fareedh's suggestion. She was also in the workshop, going by the equipment in the background. Peter's hair was sleep-tousled. Fareedh looked refreshed and put together, jet hair pulled back and glossy. I kind of missed his shorter, poofy hair, even if his ponytail was nice, too. Pinky…looked like Pinky. Eyespot swirls on a pink, rubbery canvas.

Marta went on. "The digital sections are pictures, as you thought, Pinky." Her floating holo head looked at me. "And you were right, Kitra. The key was figuring out what dimensions the digital matrix was supposed to have." She chuckled and looked proud. "Actually, the ship's *sayar* wasn't able to figure it out itself. It processed a dozen possible configurations, but none of them produced anything intelligible. To it, anyway. But then I saw this one."

Another display popped up above Marta's holo: a monochrome rectangle with two irregular splotches, each one roughly centered on their half of the display. Their outline struck me as familiar, somehow.

"Of course, you all know what that is," she prompted.

"Oh, sure," Pinky said without a pause. A moment later, a display above him materialized: a globe of the planet we were on. As I watched, it distorted itself, taking on the same rectangular dimensions as Marta's display so that all sections of the world were visible, albeit distorted by the projection. I could see how the ship's *sayar* had missed it, the spherical contours being markedly different from the flat ones. I would have figured it out eventually, though, and I was impressed that Marta had, too.

"A world map!" Peter exclaimed.

Marta beamed, the effect only slightly dampened by her tired, shiny eyes. "Right. And once I had that, I was able to decode the others. Well, not decode, but you know what I mean."

Fareedh murmured, "Let's see 'em."

Immediately, a handful of displays ballooned above their floating heads. I looked from one to another, trying to discern meaning, but while they clearly had formed shapes of some kind, without a reference, they could have been anything from a city map to pictures of a fungus culture.

That sank us into a pondering silence. I looked back at the display of the world map, the one Marta had used to unlock the digital code. It was monochrome, but the land masses weren't mere outlines. They were shaded, and I thought at first that they might represent topographical features. But the shading didn't match any of the mountain ranges I remembered seeing. Instead, the dark texturing was most pronounced at points on the coasts, irregularly concentrated in clumps. I zoomed in on the cluster that corresponded to the city we were in. There wasn't a grid of streets or any physical features, just what looked like a little tower made of dots. I counted six of them. Smaller towers sprouted nearby. Not a physical map, then, but some kind of political map. Were these population figures?

Or death counts?

A chill ran up my spine as my brain rushed to a conclusion. The balls in the library had all been unique. But the hundreds of balls we'd found at the outdoor and indoor kiosks had all been identical to each other. And the aliens didn't have *sayars* or their equivalent. If they were going to get news, it might be in physical form, like the old newspapers I'd read about in history books, or that were still published on some of the more reactionary Midworlds.

Maybe this was the last news dropped before everyone died. Reporting on something, a disease or a gas, that was killing everyone on the planet, dramatically enough that even the squarehead enemies on the other continent couldn't keep it a secret, given that the digital towers were on both continents.

"Armageddon," I whispered.

"What's that?" Marta asked.

"A final war. They took each other out."

Peter spoke, "Wouldn't we have seen, I dunno, blown up cities? Radiation?"

Fareedh said in his low drawl, "Not all wars are fought the same." The background shifted, suggesting he had leaned forward in his seat. "But we don't know yet if they're all dead on this continent."

A wave of nausea began at my core, spreading slowly outward. I knew what we'd have to do to confirm Fareedh's speculation.

"It doesn't make sense," Pinky was saying. His voice had taken on that lifeless quality that always scared me. "Why would they kill everyone? No one to remember." He trailed off.

I saw Fareedh give him a comforting hug. "Maybe they didn't mean to. Maybe it was some kind of killer bug that got loose and struck them all at once."

"Surely, one side would have a cure!" Peter was indignant.

Marta shook her head. "All it takes is a mutation. That it happened so quickly suggests it was tailored, too. None of them were immune." Her voice faltered.

Decision won over fear, and I checked the local time. The sun had risen an hour ago.

"I'm going to take *Majera* up. It's probably hopeless, but we should at least be sure." I waved my hand across the displays, folding them out of existence, and shrugged on yesterday's clothes.

Launch +42

We inspected three cities from a height, just to be sure. All the same, except in the others, there hadn't been any robots to tidy things up. On the other continent, the people had had some kind of warning. We had found most of them in shelters of some kind. Here, death had spread without notice. If we'd seen this scene first, we might have avoided the whole mess with the machines. No, we'd have checked out those power and infrared signatures regardless.

With acid in my throat, I hit the sticks, putting distance between us and the last city as quickly as possible. The horizon careened as we slew sideways and out, but there was no sensation of movement. Just the lurch in my stomach from a completely different cause.

The sun was high in the sky at that point, its glare dimmed automatically by the Window. Dully, I stole a glance at our fuel gauge. We were under 50%. It was ironic. Thanks to Peter, we could now bridge ten light years at a time using virtually no gas. But just flitting around in the air had used up half of our hydrogen. Of course, it made sense. Brute force resisting of gravity using just the thrusters was the least efficient way to travel, even if it was the most convenient.

"I'm going to find a place to tank up," I said. My voice was arid.

"Some place far away from everything." I heard a shiver in Marta's voice.

I piloted the ship over the jagged spine that divided the continent almost in two. I deliberately avoided the gray ribbons of road that ran into the mountains, searching for the remotest section of the rough country. The peaks below were tall and sharp, occasionally salted with snow. After a few minutes of searching, I found what I was looking for: an alpine lake. A quick flash of deep radar showed no artificial structures and no pavement.

Down we went. The ground was as uneven at the local level as it had been throughout the range, but I found a rocky beach broad enough for us to seat the ship. I left the thrusters primed for a moment, even after we'd touched down, to make sure the gravel could hold our weight. It did, the view from the Window barely jarring as we settled onto the pebbles.

We had hardly spoken since we'd left for the range. No one did now. Peter got up from his station almost as soon as we landed, Fareedh following him. Moments later, I heard the airlock cycle, a notification flashing on my display. Restlessly, the fingertips of my right hand rubbed together as I weighed staying in the ship versus suiting up and going outside. The confines of *Majera* were suddenly unbearable.

"I'm going to go join the others," I declared suddenly, standing up.

Marta nodded. "I'll come, too."

"And me," Pinky said without hesitation.

I gave him a backward glance. "You hate suiting up."

"You're not leaving me alone!"

I managed a smile and extended my hand.

"No. Never."

Fareedh and Peter had already extruded the meter-wide fueling pipe and were hauling it toward the lake when I got outside. The contrast between here and the cities couldn't have been more stark, and I had to pause to appreciate it.

It was lovely. Ringed by frost-fringed mountains, the water was a dark, azure mirror to the sky's clear and brilliant blue. A splash made me turn, just in time to see a long winged, hot pink creature skim away from the lake, something long and struggling in its dangling tentacles. More of its kind circled above.

Dark green shrubs clung to the lower slopes before giving way to bare rock and, as my gaze traveled upward, ice. A memory stabbed at me, surprisingly clear; a starport nestled in a mountain range. I couldn't remember where or when, but it must have been one of the stops *L'émissaire* made on its many diplomatic trips when I was still traveling with my mother.

It was quiet, but not in an unnatural or spooky way. Just the kind of peace one expects in the mountains. The rustle of branches in the breeze. The occasional splash or scatter from animals and moving water. Here, hundreds of kilometers from civilization, there was welcome relief. I took a deep breath and pretended I could taste fresh alpine air. Of course, all I got was a lungful of recycled stuff. I wasn't taking off my suit and helmet for anything.

Then I had a thought, and I took a chance on voicing it. "You think *someone* might have survived? Maybe far enough away? There must be lots of places like this. Some of them might have random hikers in them or something."

Marta's voice came from behind me, "Whatever did the killing acted so quickly and so universally that there wasn't any way to escape it. I'd be surprised if whatever it is or was didn't blanket the whole planet."

I turned to look at her. Her green suit stood out against the white of *Majera*. She brushed my shoulder with gloved fingertips, whether for my reassurance or hers, I wasn't sure.

Fareedh's voice came to my ears through the suit comms, "We could do a search of the wilderness. Look for likely spots and maybe find something." He didn't sound very hopeful.

"That'd take forever," Peter said, hefting the mouth of the fuel tube into the lake, cracking through the thin rime of ice that coated the shore. "The sensors aren't sensitive enough. Any heat we find is just as likely to be from animals."

"The wind has had half a year to waft the stuff all over the planet. It even got into airtight vaults," Marta said.

I looked bleakly around the wilderness, then sat heavily on a flattened rock. I looked up, expecting Marta to join me, but she was heading toward a clump of shrubs, maybe to take a sample. From behind her, Pinky ambled up on two legs. He was wearing a utility belt with small packs clipped to the sides. He sat down next to me and began rummaging through one of the bags.

"What have you got there?" I asked.

"I had an idea. We got more than just the news balls. Now that Marta's cracked the digital code, I thought I might see if the other ones we got had pictures." He gripped his *sayar* in one hand, dug out a ball with another. He popped up a display between us so I could see it as easily as he could. Blurs of waveforms rushed by in glowing streams as he ran the finger of a third hand along the artifact's surface.

Pinky quickly found a digital patch, the pink and yellow squiggles suddenly resolving into phosphorescent shapes. I looked at Pinky and found his eyespots were facing me. I shrugged. The holos were as meaningless as the ones we'd seen before, except for the map.

The whole ball had just four picture bits, none of them comprehensible. He put the thing back in his empty pack and dug a new one out of the other. Patiently, he set to work again. It was the same routine, the sheet music of lines whizzing by, punctuated by Rorschach images. These were somehow more angular than the other ones, but nevertheless just as random.

"I wonder if we're just not seeing them the way they did," I suggested.

"Who knows? Maybe they were really into abstract art." Pinky dropped the read ball into the other pouch and withdrew a third.

I heard Marta trudging around on the rocks and looked up. She was stuffing soil into sample tubes a few meters away. The boys were still wrestling with the fuel hose. I looked back down at the display.

My breath caught. The series of concentric rings around a central orb was impossible to mistake.

"A solar system map!" I exclaimed. Pinky said much the same thing at the same time.

Seven rings girdling a dot. Could that be this system? What other system could it be? It's not like the Pesadumbrans could have gotten anywhere else. Sure, our observations had only confirmed the five we had charted before Jumping here, but the outer two would have been harder to spot without doing a full sky survey.

I called up our system map stored in the ship's *sayar*. My heart sank. They didn't line up. Then I realized the map on the ball might have been done in logarithmic scale so all the orbits could appear in one frame; a true representation of distance would have pushed all but the first three planets off of the map. I adjusted for that, and suddenly the match was perfect. The large gap between planets three and four settled it.

I pored over the display hungrily. The seventh planet would have been invisible from Pesadumbre without a telescope. For it to be on the map meant the aliens had developed a decent degree of astronomy. I zoomed in and found the resolution of the map surprisingly high. Each of the orbits had a world depicted with its true relative size. There were circles around the outer planets, too: moons, including some truly tiny ones. Even more significantly, there was a little star above the second planet as well as a smaller one above the first. Those couldn't be moons, since neither world had any.

"Guys," I said. "I think the aliens had spaceflight. Beyond orbital, I mean"

"You're looking at those little asterisks?" Pinky asked.

"Yeah."

Marta had joined us. Fareedh and Peter were heading over from the shore, fuel pipe forgotten for the moment.

I said excitedly, "These stars must mean something. Plus, they knew about those outer moons. A lot of them wouldn't be visible to the ground, probably not even from orbit."

Peter arrived and asked, his voice a little breathy, "You think they sent probes to other planets?"

I nodded. "Maybe crewed ships!"

Fareedh, right behind him, said, "Hmm. There were hardly any satellites in orbit when we got here, though. You'd think that would be the first step in an advanced space program. Lots of satellites, I mean"

Marta added, "And we know they've got the ability to launch things into orbit. They've got those missiles."

"Maybe they were too small for us to pick up," Peter suggested.

Fareedh shook his head. "They'd have to be pretty tiny not to be visible. At sunrise or sunset, satellites reflect the light and show up as little stars, steadily moving."

"Unless," Pinky said, "they're designed to be hard to spot."

Peter spread out his hands. "Or maybe they were all shot down."

"Or both," Pinky said.

I broke in, "The important thing is that they had some kind of space travel."

"Limited, chemical type stuff, probably," Peter replied. "They didn't even have fusion."

"They didn't have to go to another star," I said, getting excited.

"There are two inhabitable planets in this system!"

Things went quiet. Peter stood with his mouth open. Fareedh's eyes took on a faraway look.

"I didn't detect signs of civilization in Planet One's atmosphere, though," Marta said. She wasn't arguing, just commenting.

"Sure, and that's why we came here first," I said. "But space travel probably is a fairly new thing here. If they went to the first planet, it couldn't have been too long ago."

Peter folded his arms. "Even if they did some kind of landing, it couldn't have been long term."

Pinky stood up, his rubbery skin hot pink with excitement. "Why not? Humans took as long as they did to leave their home planet because none of the others in the system could be lived on. My people didn't even *know* there were any other planets. But these folks, they spent their whole history knowing there was a nearby world with plants and life, the right temperature. If they could go there, they would, and they'd make plans to stay."

"Unless the air was poison," Marta said. "Unless the biosphere was too incompatible. A million unlesses."

Fareedh spoke up, resonance returning to his low voice, "Have we got anything better to do than check it out?"

I felt my heart pounding in my ears, and now I was standing. "This disaster was recent. That colony on the first planet…"

"…*if* there is one," Peter countered.

"There's an asterisk there for a reason! It might need supplies. Guys, if this is anything like with the Émilie, time is of the essence. Oh, I wish we'd gone there first!"

"We couldn't have known," Fareedh said. "But you're right. The sooner we check it out, the better." He tugged at Peter's arm, leading him back to the intake tube, which was useless until it was hooked up.

"But how will we find them?" Pinky asked. "There can't be too many people there, and if it's a small settlement, it won't easily be found from orbit." Then he pulsed yellow a couple of times and made a show of knuckling the clear pane of his suit above his eye spots, complete with what sounded just like rapping on hollow wood. "Oh, of course. The ball," he said, digging it out. "It has lots of pictures. I bet one of them is a map of Planet One."

I watched as he repeated the routine from before, running his fingers over the artifact while projecting the output onto a display. One by one, a set of holos floated above him, blocking the laboring Fareedh and Peter from sight. Marta stayed to watch, too.

Then Pinky threw out another display, this one a fuzzy globe — a shot of planet Number One we'd taken from orbit, I quickly gathered.

"We got the better part of a complete Planet One day while we were coming here," Marta said. "We should have a full map, or close to it."

"Yup," Pinky said. The image of Planet Number One peeled like a fresh purple and then distended to a rectangular shape, mottled gray and brown with no polar cap. My eyes darted from this new map to the floating displays. Pinky quickly found the picture from the ball that matched and superimposed one of them onto ours, lining up the edges.

And now, near the edge of one of the darker patches was, no joke, a big "X", marking…something. It took everything I had in me not to say, "Yar, mateys. Let's go find us some buried treasure!"

They wouldn't have gotten it anyway.

Chapter Ten

Launch +43

"You know, you really need to start thinking about what spells you want to research after you hit 500 skill points," Pinky was saying, materializing a holo of my S&S character sheet. "You should hit that target after you reach the Purple Shrine."

I flopped back on my bunk and blinded myself with the crook of my elbow. "After all we went through on that planet, you're still worried about your campaign?"

Pinky sounded affronted. "Meryem the Blessed is an important part of the party, Kitra."

My arm dropped to the bed, and I got up on my other elbow. "I've kind of had my mind on other stuff. I feel like we've got enough real adventure coming up."

He stared at me impassively. Then he asked patiently, "Remember when you got waylaid by the Flerks, and you had to go all the way back to Eragor to dress Ukko's wounds? All you needed was a good Resist Fire chant. I just don't want that to happen again."

A flash of irritation brought a sharp reply to my lips. I fought it down and studied Pinky for a moment. I couldn't read him at all. His swirly eyespots gave no hint as to what was going on behind that pink, featureless skin. But something was bothering him.

"What's going on here?" I asked, trying to smile. "Is this some kind of metaphor for what we're about to do on Planet One, and you want me to be prepared?"

He tinged yellow at that, but his words didn't register the disapproval I'd expected. "It doesn't have anything to do with the aliens.

We haven't talked about anything but that for days. I wanted to talk about something else for a change. And I wanted to be with you."

I blinked. Slowly, I replied, "I guess I've kept to myself more since that first day."

Pinky nodded his nubbin of a head. "Or you've had company. I didn't want to disturb you."

"You can always disturb me..." I began.

"Connections are important," he countered. "I am glad you are spending time with Marta. I know you are having important conversations, like the ones Peter and Marta have."

I felt myself blushing. Then I smirked. "And like Peter and Fareedh have been having."

"Yes," he said seriously. "They have been excluding me, too. Not all the time, but sometimes." He came close to the bed and extended two of his arms. "I just wanted to have a conversation with you, too."

I sat up and threw my arms around my friend. "I'm sorry. I've been neglecting you."

"You have been busy, and you have been hurting," he said, the breath coming from his flank tickling my cheek. "Today, you weren't doing anything, so I wanted to see you. That's all."

"Okay," I said, pressing away from him but keeping hands on his shoulders, or at least, where the arms around me joined with his body. "Okay. I'm all yours. Let's talk about Meryam."

He flushed a deep rose, and, as if he'd been waiting for me to say that, immediately popped up five displays, all crammed with custom notes, doodles, and arcane sub-headings. "Right. So, here are some of your options..."

We were about halfway through Holy Trap Detection prayers when the door chimed. I waved the portal open, and it was Fareedh, dressed in shorts and a top that looked like a supernova had exploded in rainbow.

"Oh hey. Hope I'm not interrupting," he said tentatively.

I looked over at Pinky, but he waved Fareedh in cheerfully. "Well, some of this stuff is Top Secret," he said conspiratorially, "but you'll find out soon enough." He turned hot pink. "Hey! Want to talk about Lionel?"

A flicker of confusion crossed Fareedh's dark features before his eyes widened in comprehension. "Oh! Ah, yes, but, let's stick a tab on that one. I was actually hoping to talk to Kitra for a quick second." He looked at me with less of his confident air than usual.

Pinky seemed to deflate slightly, but he kept his tinge neutrally pink and said, cheerfully, "No problem. I've kept her for a while. But we need to talk about Lionel's issue with climbing walls soon..."

"You got it, pal. Promise to do it before we go home."

Mollified, Pinky got up from where he'd been seated pretzel-legged on the brown rug that carpeted about half of my stateroom floor. I gave him a kiss on his stumpy noggin, and for good measure, Fareedh did, too, and that made his pink skin flush a little deeper. He padded out the door. It slid shut behind him.

Fareedh looked a question at me.

I shrugged. "I think he's just lonely. And maybe depressed. You remember how he got on the Émilie."

"Yeah, I'm surprised he hasn't started walking in circles again."

The memory flashed vividly: Pinky and Fareedh exploring the mortally wounded colony ship surrounded by thousands of sleeping—and some dead—exiles from Gloire. Pinky solemnly walking in a ring through the circular deck, paying some kind of tribute to them. I still didn't fully understand his meaning, and I hadn't wanted to pry.

"I think he just wanted to get his mind off of things. We'll be reaching Number One in..." I took a quick look at my *sayar*, then grimaced. "Lord, just seven hours." Pinky and I had been chatting for almost four hours. No wonder my throat felt scratchy.

"You guys were talking S&S stuff?" he asked.

"Kind of. There was a lot of reminiscing, too. In game and otherwise."

"That's cool. Sometimes I envy your connection. You've known him a long time."

"You two have gotten pretty close, too. You're always making games together and playing chess and stuff."

He ran a hand over his pulled back hair. "Oh sure. But it hasn't been a decade."

"I guess that's true." I leaned back, backward palms pressed flat against my bunk. "So what's up?"

Fareedh glanced at the cabin's one chair, and I nodded. He sat in his typical style, on his knees rather than his behind.

"I guess I just wanted to check up on you. We hadn't seen you since we left Two...er... Pesadumbre."

I glanced down at the rug. "We probably should have been doing more planning this whole trip, huh? We wasted the day."

He shook his head. "I'm not too worried. We're kind of waiting on more data anyway."

"Still, I probably didn't need to spend so much time sleeping and then blathering." I looked up at him again. "I take it you guys have been more responsible?"

Fareedh did something I rarely saw: he blushed. "Well, I don't know if I'd say that."

I made a show of rolling my eyes and sighing. "You and Peter at it again, huh?" I wanted to show how in-the-know and blasé I was. "Where was Marta during all of this? Working on her plants? I figured she had to be, or she would have commed or come over."

Fareedh's flush deepened. "Where do you think she was?" he replied.

"I don't.. oh. Wait, all day? With you guys? But I thought... I mean, with you and Peter being... Oh Lord." I buried my face in my hands, and from the heat, I could tell *I* was blushing.

"Marta said she'd explained things." Fareedh's voice came from closer. I looked through my fingers and saw he had come down to kneel on the floor in front of me. "About us, I mean."

"Kind of," I admitted. "I guess I just figured since she and I were back together, and you and Peter seemed so happy, that, we'd just... I dunno."

"Paired off?" he offered.

I nodded. "Yeah. I mean, she said she and Peter were still a thing, and I guess I knew that in theory, but... well, you know. Like Professor Malas used to say, 'In theory, practice and theory are the same, but in practice they're different.'" It was a dumb saying, which is probably why I remembered it.

"It's sort of becoming a group thing," Fareedh went on, his smile now more impish than shy. "Peter has good taste."

"How long has it been, ah, the three of you?"

"Well, it was always sort of an open option, you know? But today was the first day it really congealed."

Gah. My brain was reeling, trying to reconfigure its framework to see my shipmates not just as friends, but as lovers. I didn't want to know more. No, that's not true. I *did* want to know.

"All day?!"

He nodded. "We were having fun."

I tried to laugh it off. "And I wasn't invited?"

His look became more serious in a flash. "You'd have been welcome," he said. "After before, I didn't want to press."

My mouth opened, then shut. I waved a hand in front of me, "Hold on. I need to process. Just a second."

He nodded and gestured, palms up, giving me space. I shut my eyes and thought. Okay. Fareedh and Peter, going out. Maybe more than that. Got it. Marta and Peter still going out. Yep. Of course. That was as natural as hydrogen and oxygen. OK. Stop. How did that feel? Honestly? It had always bugged me a little, like maybe I'd never mattered at all. Well, how about now? Yes. In fact, the ember flamed to life as I thought about them spending the day together. Just as quickly, my jealousy flickered out. She hadn't kept anything from me. She'd told me the score. And she certainly hadn't been holding back on our time together. If anything, she'd been depriving Peter lately.

So, that was fine, I guess. But now, add Fareedh to the Peter and Marta thing. Or was it adding Marta to the Peter and Fareedh thing?

I shook my head, so hard I felt my pony tail fly against my shoulders.

"Too much?" Fareedh asked.

"Yeah."

"I'll keep quiet."

"No, it's okay. So you…you didn't tell me because you were trying to be respectful? Because I shot you down back on the Émilie?"

He nodded, dark eyes wide and uncharacteristically grave.

"I felt bad. You really have been great about it."

"I understood," he said, just the tiniest tinge of pain under the empathy.

"But you wanted me there, today?"

He brightened. "We all did. You're still invited." He hesitated. "If you're interested, I mean."

I glanced at the wall, Fareedh's handsome face suddenly too much to look at. Marta, I knew. We'd been a thing. Getting back together had felt natural, more natural than it had been the first time. And I was pretty sure I could be fine with sharing, being at sort of the edge of things. But being with all of them? Three fourths of my best friends? *With* them?

I tried to recalibrate, wrestling with the idea of Fareedh and Peter being *my* lovers. Fareedh, sure. I'd thought about that a lot until we tried to put that into practice at exactly the wrong time. But Peter? He was conventionally handsome, I guess, if you liked them built like Greek Gods. But he was *Peter*. Not only was that synonymous with "Marta's boyfriend", but Peter was a complainer. A coward. I called him "Mouse" for a reason.

Except... was that really Peter anymore? Not for months, I realized. The Peter I knew now was fearless, and selfless, and really nice. Marta *did* have good taste. And Fareedh.

I stole a glance back at Fareedh, who smiled, his eyes widening in a momentary flash, a gesture just as attractive as ever. I looked away, heat in my cheeks. No, I didn't have trouble seeing Fareedh as a potential partner.

But just like on the Émilie, now was a stressful time. And we weren't just talking about ten thousand refugees, but the fate of millions of aliens. Why did things like this have to come up at the dumbest moments?

I cleared my throat and asked, "What does 'invited' mean?"

"Whatever you feel comfortable with," he said gently. His eyes began to glisten. "We all love you, you know."

Something compelled me to put my hand on his. It was warm under its sharp contours.

"I love you, too," I found myself saying. "It's just a lot to think about."

He nodded without words.

I glanced at my *sayar* on the bunk, the display bobbing above it. "And I've, *we've*, got to get some sleep before we make orbitfall. Otherwise, we won't be able to do the strategic planning I'm supposed to be heading up."

"I guess that is the priority, isn't it?"

"For now," I agreed. I managed a little smile. "But I promise I will think about it. About us, I mean. I'm not…I'm not saying no." Good Lord. Was this really happening?

My hand began to tremble, and Fareedh put his other on top of it, clasping my fingers between his.

"It'll be alright. Whatever happens." He gave my hands a squeeze, then stood up and gave a sloppy salute. "We'll report for duty at oh-five-hundred, Captain."

I snorted, my smile broadening. I saluted him back, crisply, as I'd seen in countless holos and space romances. "Dis*missed*!" I said.

Then I flopped, back-first on my bed after the door closed and stared at the ceiling for a good, long time.

Chapter Eleven

Launch +44

The first planet of the system was a mottled, beige sphere that filled about a tenth of the Window. Pinky had "parked" us in a geostationary orbit 43,000 kilometers above its surface, our trip around the planet matching the world's 30-hour day. We seemed to hang suspended above the sunlit hemisphere, only the slowly creeping shadow of night at the far end of the planet's disc betraying our movement.

It wasn't a pretty world. Only a few clouds scudded across the overwhelming expanse of land. There was none of the green of life, though there were ragged patches of grayish brown. I couldn't tell yet if these were fields of vegetation, scum-filled seas, or plains of cooled lava. It was hard to believe that our aliens could have found refuge here.

But the bright double edge to the planet showed that there was an atmosphere, and Marta had reported plenty of oxygen. There had to be life down there. Maybe it was all on the back side. No, that was silly. We'd observed a full rotation of the planet on the 31-hour trip here. Our far side holo was a little blurrier, but it didn't look much different.

I upped the magnification, sweeping our view across swathes of tan and olive. It wasn't a concerted search or anything, just a quick survey on the off chance that an obvious settlement would spring into view. It didn't. Just a lot of dingy plains, plateaus, and mountain ranges. I zoomed in on a dark patch. It was flat and featureless.

"That's plants," Marta's voice said firmly from behind me. Her tone softened, "Infrared absorption and oxygen production suggest it, anyway."

"We get anything on comms?" I asked.

"Dead air on normal channels. There's a decent roar of atmospherics, which I guess is to be expected. We're closer to the star, and the atmosphere's thick enough for a lot of ionization."

"So we couldn't tell if they were broadcasting, anyway," Pinky said. "At least in the old radio bands."

I swiveled to face the gang. "What do you think? Do we risk deep radar? I can't imagine they've set up a missile system, if they'd even notice a deep radar scan."

"If they're even here," Peter added.

Fareedh leaned forward in his chair. "Let's do it," he urged gently.

I unzoomed the display and activated the scan. The Window automatically shifted to the deep radar spectrum, and the planet turned into a surreal picture of itself: the ground showed up in shades of glowing yellow, the seas turned to charcoal—perhaps they were water after all. I eyed the disk for the tell-tale brown of metal and plastic.

Nothing.

"Maybe they built their homes out of stone," Marta suggested.

Peter replied, "Yeah, but their spaceship wasn't made out of rocks."

"We could just be on the wrong side of the planet," Fareedh suggested. "There may just be the one…"

A *ping* cut him off, and a pink ring popped up on the display close to the lower edge of the world. "Reflection detected," appeared next to it. The ship's *sayar* had found what our eyes weren't keen enough to resolve.

I asked the ship's *sayar* for a close-up, both in deep radar and visual. The Window split into two displays and zoomed in, a little scale marker overlaying both. At a field of about a kilometer across, it became obvious what we'd found. In the left display, a yellow plain dominated by a glowing pink cylinder ringed by subtle brown irregularities. On the right, the same cylinder was done in black and white checkers, and the circle of brown clumps resolved into neat houses, all of them round. From the reflections and colors, they were made from a mix of native materials and metal or synthetics

In visible light, the ground didn't have that same beige pallor. Instead, it was sort of a splotchy blue. The splotches were regularly spaced, circular, and they spread out a fair ways from the grounded ship. I stared for a bit, trying to figure out why. Pools of some kind? No, they'd be green. Then I caught myself, remembering that the oceans of Sirena were blue, and also on Pesadumbre. I was still shaking Vatanian habits.

"I think those are fields," Marta said. "For crops, I mean."

"Weren't the plants on 'Two' green?" Peter asked.

"Maybe they're covered. The sunlight is more intense here."

Pinky spoke up, "Hey, I think there's movement." His voice was calm, but I saw him flush with excitement.

There was nothing in the deep radar display, but on the right, there were shimmerings alongside the homes, the blue circles. At first, I thought they might be artifacts of distance, but they moved regularly — little dots, like hivers around a nest. My heart leaped, as my eyes darted from the right display to the left. Still nothing on deep radar. If they'd been metal robots, like the ones we'd run into before, they'd have shown up.

I tried upping the magnification, but that just gave me a blown up blur. "Fareedh," I said. "Can you increase the resolution?"

He tsked his teeth in a negative. "We'll just get magnified distortion. If we want a better look, we'll have to get closer."

I glanced at the fuel display. Our gas was at 73%.

"It's not too much fuel, Kitra," Pinky reassured. "I can put us in a 90-minute orbit, and we can do a flyover."

I smiled and gave him a pat on his leftmost paw. He'd read my mind. 73% was normally plenty, especially with Peter's new Drive. But if there wasn't any free water down there, we could get pretty close to our safety margin landing and taking off again, at least if we just used thrusters. Every cubic milliliter of hydrogen was valuable. Every orbital shift cost fuel.

Plus, every fiber in me wanted to just land *Majera* right now. If the aliens were in trouble...

Well, they didn't *look* like they were in trouble, at least from here. I reminded myself that it was always valuable to get more information before plunging headlong into danger. For all I knew, one of those "homes" was a missile emplacement.

"Okay," I conceded. "Take us lower."

"Sure, Tuessa designs are fine," Fareedh was saying, "but Courrèges really makes a line."

"You don't think his stuff bunches too much?" I heard Marta reply, her tone skeptical.

"Well, it bunches in the right places for *me*," he said playfully. "And I've got a friend who does custom alterations. That helps a lot."

"Oh of course. You can't leave that kind of thing to a Maker."

I restrained a sigh and took another bite from the plate of orzo rice Pinky had handed me. It was simple, but good, and hand-made. Or pseudopod-made. He got the chicken and spinach balance right. It used to surprise me that he got human tastes down so well given the weird stuff he "drank", but he was probably the best cook on the ship now. Maybe it was because he could taste what he was preparing with his fingers.

That should have grossed me out a lot more than it did. I guess we'd been friends too long.

I let Fareedh and Marta's discussion of fashion wash over me, watching the Window idly from our new vantage. The planet was no more beautiful for being close up, but at least it had some variety. We were currently sailing over one of the flat stretches of slate that Marta and our instruments said was a sea. It seemed weird that the planet had so many isolated bodies of water rather than more defined oceans and continents, like I was used to. Of course, there were plenty of worlds without standing water at all, and some, one-faced worlds like Punainen, that had most of their moisture locked up in ice on the frozen night side.

If we ever made planetary surveying our business, it probably wouldn't hurt to learn geology. Or add a geologist to the team.

Pinky tapped my hand and then pointed. "The site should be coming over the limb, now. We'll get a nice view. We're just a few hundred kilometers up."

I watched where he was pointing and saw glowing arrows marking a spot just over the gently curved horizon. It had taken a little while to get here. Instead of just dropping us straight in, Pinky had plotted a fuel-conscious maneuver that first put us in an eccentric orbit, shedding altitude quickly, and then made our path circular again with a burn when we were at the right height. I could have done it, too; I had the math. But Pinky was the navigator, as good at real-space maneuvers as he was at hyperspace plots. That's why he got to sit up front. He could probably even land the ship, provided we didn't need anything fancy.

The sea below us didn't end, exactly, but merged with the beige ground. It was a really flat world, I realized. From a low orbit over most planets, you can make out mountain ranges and valleys, canyons and wadis. There was hardly any of that here. On the other hand, the surface wasn't entirely uniform, with darker streaks of brown relieving the monotony. In a few spots, I saw circular features that looked a bit like craters, but without high rims. One was filled with the seawater gray.

And then the site was over the planet's edge, 2,000 kilometers away and closing fast. The view zoomed in, automatically compensating for *Majera's* motion, even though we were racing along at seven kilometers per second. It still wasn't a very clear view yet. We were much closer, but we were also looking through the atmosphere sideways, blurring everything. In fact, I could only make out the site in deep radar. In the visible spectrum, the zoomed-in display was just a shimmer of tan.

"Can you give us a wider view?" Peter asked. Pinky obliged. I exclaimed a little "oh", as it became obvious what was obscuring our vision.

A dust storm, hundreds of kilometers wide. At a distance, it had blended in with the terrain, but magnified, it ran and shifted like a living thing, darker tendrils within its broad body. There was no telling when it had sprung up. It must have been going for a while, it was so large. And it had enveloped the alien settlement.

"We'll have to fly through that stuff," I said, nose wrinkling. It probably wouldn't hurt the ship, but who knew?

"They have to *live* in that stuff," Marta observed.

Fareedh said wryly, "Hey, we've got wind and dust back on Vatan, too."

"Not both at the same time," Peter said.

"True."

"We could wait out the storm," Pinky said. "But..."

"But we don't know how long it's going to last," I objected. "I don't want to just sit in orbit if time is of the essence."

Marta came up and put a hand on my shoulder and looked at the rapidly closing landing site. "If you can land in that storm, there may be a good side to this."

"What's that?"

"We don't know if they're going to be friendly or not, or whether they might be terrified of something coming out of the sky. For all they know, they might think we're the enemy coming to finish them off." She looked down at me and smiled. "The dust will give us cover. We can land, get close, and figure out what to do without them noticing us."

I pursed my lips and considered the expanse of roiling beige before answering. "I was going to break orbit and do a gliding reentry to save fuel." I had the ship's *sayar* measure the cloud tops. They went up to about 3,000 meters. "I guess I could do that most of the way in and then drop us straight down using thrusters. The air will have bled off most of our velocity by then. As long as the ground is solid, I could land using deep radar or infrared. Oh! Let's see if we can see *them* in infrared." I mentally kicked myself for not thinking of that before.

But changing the display to detect in the wavelengths of heat, beyond the red end of the spectrum that human eyes could see, didn't tell us much. In fact, the dots we'd seen higher up weren't even visible now. Either they didn't show up in infrared or, more likely, they had taken shelter.

We weren't going to learn much more until we landed.

Manual landings are about my favorite thing in the universe. There's just something primal about gliding on wind, even the almost vacuum a hundred kilometers up, as opposed to just letting the antigrav take you down like a cargo lift. Plus, it uses a lot less fuel. Friction as the ship hits the air does the braking for you.

I flared *Majera* up, letting the heat of reentry spread out over as much of the ship's belly as possible, and also to cut our speed quickly. The deceleration pulled me into my seat, not at the full ten gees it would have been without antigrav, but just enough so I could *feel* each turn and speed change — not just see it on my displays. That was Fareedh and Pinky's doing: we could have nullified the gees entirely, but that would have been like flying with earplugs and foggles for me. With the program the two had put into the ship's *sayar*, the ship felt more like my old, engineless glider and less like a 200-ton spacecraft.

It worked for me. I don't know if anyone else has rigged their ship the same way.

In no time, I was yawing *Majera* around, stubby wings biting into the thin but substantial air about ten kilometers up. We were no longer reentering, but soaring. Our fuel was still above 65% and hardly dropping at all. My smile faded as I looked below in visual light. Wisps of dust drifted not far beneath us, and below that, a seething cauldron in shades of brown. It wasn't rational to be worried. It wasn't like the particles could get inside the ship, which was necessarily sealed against air as well as the vacuum of space. As long as I didn't have our air scoops open, we should be fine. I was uneasy, anyway.

I spiraled us in over the site, navigating by deep radar to make sure I knew our altitude precisely. If our determination of the ground height was even a meter off, we'd plow into the dirt, and that'd be that. At 2,000 meters, the ground was completely obscured in the visible light spectrum. I cut in the thrusters and dropped us into the storm.

After the first lurch, I shut off the antigrav program. We weren't soaring anymore, just plunging straight down, and we didn't need to feel every gust of wind. Still, the strength of the storm was obvious, both from the thrust we had to spend to keep us steady, and also from the sensors. At times, the gale rose to 120 kilometers per hour. If it was this strong at the surface, we'd have to shelter inside like the aliens. There's no way we could stay upright against that kind of blast. I wondered how the alien houses stood it.

"Not too close," Peter cautioned. "We don't want to land on top of them."

"We also don't want to have to go too far in this," I said, but I angled us farther away from the ship that marked the center of the alien site. Deep radar showed a couple of low hills on one side of those mysterious blue circles. That'd be some cover, at least. In infrared, I saw a curious ring around the settlement, enclosing both the ponds/ fields and the homes. It was thin, so it hadn't been visible until now, and there wasn't much detail even this close up. I made sure to aim outside of that, too.

At five meters up, according to the deep radar, I put down the landing skids. I eased the ship down very slowly, my hands slick as I watched the altimeter drop decimal by decimal. Green lights popped up as the hull registered solid ground on the skids, and I cut the thrusters. Our height stayed steady. I sat back and exhaled.

Then I swiveled to face the others. "Now what?"

Pinky jerked an oversized thumb at the Window. "Do we wait for that to clear?" The view outside was just endless, impenetrable, shimmers of sand.

"What's the wind speed?" Fareedh asked softly.

Pinky answered, "About 50 kilometers per hour. Gusts could be higher."

"That doesn't sound too bad," Fareedh said.

"It's not the wind," Peter countered. "It's what the wind is blowing."

I looked over my shoulder at the display. I didn't think dust could get into our suits, but a few whizzing rocks at nearly 100 kilometers an hour would sting, if not outright puncture. Pinky's suit was made of stiffer stuff, as we saw on Pesadumbre, but I wasn't about to send him out on his own.

"Why don't we wait for things to die down a bit," I suggested. "The aliens will probably ride out the storm indoors, so we wouldn't be able to talk to them anyway."

"Won't we lose the cover of the storm?" Peter asked.

"We're going to have to show ourselves sometime," Marta pointed out. "This was just so they wouldn't see us land." I nodded agreement and turned to the Window for a moment, putting the view in infrared. The dust disappeared, for the most part. The hill we were behind was bigger than I'd thought, blocking our view of the alien settlement. Good. If we couldn't see them, they couldn't see us.

"What do we do in the meantime?" Marta asked.

Pinky raised a hand and his voice. "Starships and Supernovas!"

"Are you kidding?" Peter didn't look amused.

"Yes."

"Eat? Drink? Bathroom break?" I offered.

Fareedh stifled a yawn. "Nap?"

Peter gave him a gentle shove. "You can sleep?"

Fareedh shrugged. "I can always sleep."

I got up out of my chair, half-expecting to be stuck to it with all the sweating I'd done during landing, but the seat, like the controls, did a good job of dealing with it. "Well, I'm going to work in reverse order on my suggestions. I've been holding it for half an hour."

I went past them to go to my cabin, a little more urgently than I'd planned. It's funny what you don't realize until after things calm down. Luckily, we all had toilet facilities built into our Cleaners. The privacy was nice. A good 60 seconds of quiet and no blinkety lights.

When I was done, I left my room and saw everyone was in the wardroom but Fareedh. Peter said without me asking about it, "He really is taking a nap," with not a little exasperation.

"Guess you shouldn't have worn him out," I said, the words out of my mouth before I realized it. Peter flushed as only someone with his pale coloration can. I looked away contritely and caught sight of Jub-Jub's tank. I figured it could use some company, so I opened the enclosure top and stuck my arms in. As it eagerly wound its spindly arms around my wrists, I heard Peter say, "I'm not the one who wears him out."

I looked up to see Peter eyeing Marta significantly. She looked innocently at him, then at me. Jealousy and commiseration warred within me for a moment. Sympathy won out. Marta was a tigress.

Pinky shaded a deep maroon. "What are you guys talking about?"

Marta and Peter said, "Nothing!" in unison. I coughed and then felt a little bad. Pinky was the odd man out.

"Wrestling," I said, sitting down with Jub-Jub cradled in my arms. "You know. For fun." It sounded dumb even to my ears.

"How come you don't invite me?" Before I could answer, his skin returned to normal rather suddenly. "You guys are just scared, I understand." He grew out his arms menacingly. "I'd beat you in a fair fight."

"That's fair?" Peter said incredulously.

"Not my fault your bodies are so boring."

I let out a breath and sat, my mind going kind of blank. I didn't have any plan of action, nor any more real data to use to formulate one.

"It's just kind of weird that they'd come to this place," Peter said, suddenly. "The aliens, I mean. It's just so marginal here, if it's all like this."

Marta shrugged. "It's got oxygen, and it's in the same system. That's actually pretty huge."

I nodded. Any oxygen world was something special. I thought again of Punainen, also a bleak and windy world. But it was also the closest planet with breathable air to be found on the Coreward side of the Rift from Hyvilma.

"Maybe the settlement was an emergency measure," Pinky suggested. "Like a, you know, Noah's Ark. A way to escape planetwide destruction."

That put us in a pensive silence. Eventually, Peter and Marta got up to make food while I scratched Jub-Jub's head idly. Fareedh showed up, his hair down and a bit poofy, about fifteen minutes later. As he came in, he made a point to give Pinky a hug before kissing both Peter and Marta on the back of their heads. Pinky pulsed happily. I guess he'd picked up on Pinky's loneliness, or maybe Pinky had talked to him, too.

"What's the wind like?" he asked, a plate of falafel in his hands.

I consulted my *sayar*, tied into the ship's sensors. "Oh! We're down to 30."

"Great! Let me scarf this down, and we can go out."

"You nap quick."

"It's true. How're we looking outside?

"One sec," I said and called up the Window display to see if the dust had died down. It had, but the light was still dim, dimmer than it had been. Dusk was already falling, I realized. I pursed my lips. I should have considered that. I switched to infrared, which would be unaffected by the lower light.

And gasped.

"What's wrong?" Pinky asked.

"Um, guys. Look at this," I said, expanding the display and flinging it to cover one of the walls.

Outside the ship were a dozen person-sized beings arrayed in a line, glowing brightly.

Chapter Twelve

"Infinity," Peter breathed the curse.

I turned down the contrast, and the aliens sprang into sharp relief, their forms now shades of gray shimmering with an internal fire. They wore clothes—loose-fitting *bishts* with hoods that covered their bodies. They could have been humans, but something about their posture, the placement of the shoulders, the width of the heads, said otherwise.

"They're just standing there," Marta said.

"I think they're waiting for us," said Fareedh..

I nodded, throat dry. Now that they were actually here, and surrounding us, I felt less eager to go meet them.

"I should go out there," Pinky said, already shaping his body to match the alien contours, as he had when he'd fooled the robots.

"You're not going out there alone, pal!" Peter blurted.

Pinky flushed rose, the familiar gesture odd on his spindly new form. "I was hoping you'd say that. But what if those guys don't like the look of humans?"

I put a hand on Pinky's shoulder, now in line with mine. "We'll test that pad when we come to it."

"They don't seem to be armed," Fareedh noted.

Peter shot back, "Lot of room in those robes."

"What shape are their heads?" Marta asked.

Good question. If the settlers were from the first continent, square heads might make them mad. And vice versa.

"I can't tell," I said. "The hoods cover the sides."

"The ball that had the colony on it was from that first city," Fareedh noted.

"Sure," Peter shot back. "But both sides could have landed ships by now."

"Do we play *duma duma dum*?" Pinky asked.

"You know what?" I said, "Forget random. Let's go with round heads. *Our* heads are round. Ish. Might as well be consistent. And as you said," I nodded to Fareedh, "we found out about this place from the first city."

I looked back at the display. The aliens were still standing there, eerie and ominous, long arms at their sides, and their clothes fluttering in what was still a substantial breeze.

"Let's go suit up," I said.

"In what order?" Pinky asked.

I frowned, thinking. The airlock only handled two at a time, and I wanted Pinky to have as much support as he could get. Oh! We didn't need to be *in* the lock to get dressed. We could cycle through quickly if we were already suited.

"You and me first," I said. "Then Fareedh and Marta. We'll get dressed in the cargo bay and then hurry out, two by two, so we can stay together." I stood up and began coaxing Jub-Jub back into its enclosure. For once, it didn't complain.

"You don't want me going, too?" Peter asked.

I closed the box and turned. "No."

Peter's jaw twitched, his expression hard to read.

"Look, someone's got to stay in. To watch our back, if nothing else. If it gets bad..." I swallowed, "...you can get home."

"I can't fly the ship," he protested.

"You can go up, and you can use Pinky's program to get home. Fuel's not an issue, remember?"

He frowned. "I don't like this." His gaze flickered over at Marta, then Fareedh, before returning to me. He folded his arms. "But I take your point." He followed us to the cargo bay, though.

We took turns grabbing our gear out of the airlock and then got together in the cargo bay, stripping down to underthings and getting into our suits. Pinky helped me with mine after he'd put on his special outfit. Fareedh and Marta checked each other over, making sure the tank was hooked up, the bubble extended, and all the other things you have to do before subjecting yourself to an environment that can kill you.

I noticed Marta hadn't strapped on her beamers. I didn't say any-thing.

Pinky cycled the airlock, the door opening onto a shadowy, fea-tureless view. The wind almost knocked me over as I went down the steps first. Then Pinky was toppling into me, clumsy on two legs and in an unfamiliar shape. I gripped his shoulders to brace him, and to-gether, we stepped to the ground and faced the aliens.

There were six of them. Wind whipped their untinted robes, flur-ries of dust gusting past them. Their faces were a mystery, completely in shadow. I could barely make out the bulk of the hill we'd landed behind, dim in the storm and fading twilight.

Underneath the rush of the breeze, I became aware of another sound, an almost subsonic rumble. I braced myself; this kind of noise accompanied the occasional quakes we got back home. There was no tremor beneath my feet, though. Just this pervasive, quiet roar. I bare-ly noticed the whir of the airlock cycling again, the steps of Fareedh and Marta behind me.

The rumble abruptly strengthened, though it was somehow no louder, just more intense. Six more figures shuffled from around the hull of *Majera*, falling into line with the first group.

Peter's comm made me jump, "They've all gone to your side, Kitra!"

I didn't answer, transfixed by the aliens. I didn't want to make a move, grab my *sayar*, anything that might set them off. But at the same time, I had to do something.

"What's that sound," Marta asked.

"It's coming from them, I think," Fareedh said.

Then the sound shifted, almost seeming to surround me. I shook my head, wondering if it was a pressure thing, but it persisted. I looked left, then right. It was definitely stronger on the left.

Pinky was on my left.

"Are you doing that?" I asked.

He didn't answer, but he did subtly nod his head.

The aliens, now just gray figures on deeper gray, seemed agitated. Two approached us cautiously, arms still at their sides, hoods tilted forward, as if in concentration. The rumble pulsed oddly. Then there were chirps, like the ones we'd heard in the recordings, I realized, though higher pitched and faster.

None of us said anything. Pinky continued to rumble. The chirps stopped. Now one of the aliens was reaching out for Pinky with a hand that seemed all thumbs. How Pinky managed not to flinch, I can't imagine. The strange claw explored Pinky's rounded head, splaying to palm the face plate. The alien's arm dropped, and it faced Pinky as if considering. Then the being turned to its companion, and they exchanged chirps.

"I'm recording this," Peter whispered. "I'm feeding it into the language program, too."

I nodded my head silently, afraid of disturbing the aliens with the slightest sound.

More chirps, these seeming to be directed at Pinky. He just went on rumbling. The two aliens of the vanguard turned to each other again and chittered. One of the figures in the big group called out to them, a hawk's call that pitched long and down. Both answered without turning, a reversed copy of the sound.

The alien that had touched Pinky spread its arms, the first gesture I'd seen any of them make. Pinky responded in kind, which made the other alien rock slightly on its feet. I was surprised that they could see his gesture at all, but thinking about it, if they used some kind of radar, then they'd only be blind to things without physical substance, like holos or words on a page.

The two aliens chirped to each other once more. Then they turned back and rejoined the main group, which erupted into noise. It was like the sound of the birdhouse at the zoo. Debating, I guess.

Finally, they were silent. They were dim in the nearly gone twilight, but it was clear they were leaving. All except one, who stayed behind, faced Pinky, and made the arms out gesture.

"I think they want us to follow them," Marta said, her voice low.

"I won't be able to see you if you do that." Peter sounded worried.

"Hook into the suits," Fareedh said.

"Oh, right. Okay. Monitoring. I won't have infrared, though."

The remaining alien repeated the gesture.

"Are we doing this?" Marta asked. Asking me, I guess.

I had to clear my throat before answering. "Sure."

It was now too dark to see the ground clearly, but I didn't want to startle the aliens by torching my *sayar*. Instead, I snapped my suit lights. The dim blue glow from my boots was just enough to watch my step. Luckily, the ground was pretty flat, although twice we had to dodge around organics — meter-wide, rooted swirls of stiff, broad leaves like overgrown cabbage heads.

As we rounded the hill between us and the settlement, I was faced with…nothing. Only the very dim shadow of the alien figure against an ever-so-slightly paler background. The other aliens were nowhere to be seen. I looked at Pinky in confusion, then back to the shrouded being. It spread its arms out again, then just seemed to disappear into thin air. I swallowed, then made to follow, arms outstretched like a sightless person.

My hands touched something smooth. Some kind of sheeting. I felt around the area I thought the alien had vanished into, and the material parted like a curtain. I cautiously pressed a foot through. The ground was solid on the other side, and with a lurch, I plunged onwards, leaving one hand on the opening to keep it parted for the others.

It was space-dark on this side, too. I stole a glance at the sky. Starless, as I'd expected. But the gusts had stopped, and my environment display said the particulate count was much lower. It dawned on me then: the circle surrounding the settlement was a windscreen. No wonder the beings wanted to go back behind their shelter. It couldn't have been comfortable to stand out in that driving storm for very long.

I felt Pinky sidle up beside me, and now that it was quieter, I heard Marta and Fareedh's bootsteps, crunching on the loose, sandy earth as they approached. There were other sounds, a growing rumble like the one we'd heard before, and the rustling of other beings assembling in front of us, but in the dark of the new night, they were so much mist to my eyes. There wasn't a single light on this side of the barrier.

"I can't see anything," Marta said.

"Do we chance brightening things up?" Fareedh asked.

I said, "Well, they brought us here, and they haven't pounced on us or shot us. I'll just go slow." As I spoke, I slowly reached toward my belt, unstuck my *sayar*, and torched it at low intensity. I blinked at the sudden change, then felt, rather than saw, the others in our party flinch. Whether from the light or what the light revealed, I couldn't know.

There were dozens of beings, just a few meters away, all in the same *bishts* as the ones who had come out to see us. They did not react to the light. Their hoods were all down around their necks.

They were not even remotely human.

The closest one regarded me with an unreadable face. Where a human's nose, eyes, and forehead would be, there was a smooth, round organ, like a parabolic mirror or a circular hammock. Beneath it was a slit of a mouth. There was more, but that's what I immediately registered.

On a hunch, I slowly increased the *sayar's* brightness and the torch angle until the whole area was bathed in light. No reaction from the aliens whatsoever.

"That confirms that," Marta said quietly.

"What?" Peter commed.

"They don't have eyes," Fareedh answered. "Not for the visible spectrum, anyway."

"What do they use? Radar?" Peter asked.

Pinky replied simply to that one, "Sound," without pausing his purring rumbling.

Just that one word caused several of the beings to step back, as if surprised. Two of the aliens began chittering to each other, gesturing at Pinky.

"I think Pinky's disguise just slipped," I said warily.

Fareedh shrugged. "Even if it hasn't, *we're* obviously aliens"

"We've got to find a way to communicate," Marta said. "If we could just get some reference words, the ship's *sayar* could start translating."

Fareedh watched the chittering aliens and chuckled. "I wonder if they're saying the same thing."

The fingertips of my hand slid restlessly along the smooth sides of the torched *sayar*. "Well," I said, "no time like the present. Let's try starting with the basics." I raised my free hand and said "*Selam*," in greeting, like we do on Vatan.

"Great idea," Fareedh commed under his breath. "But what if they think that's the word for 'hand'?"

"You got a better idea?" I answered testily.

A moment later, the group erupted in a chorus of chirps. To my ears, they sounded roughly the same, sort of a quick flip from high, to low, to high.

Marta commed quietly, "The soul of science is repetition." She stepped forward, raised a hand and said, "*Selam.*"

This time, the aliens responded almost in unison, and definitely with the same sound they had used before.

Peter's voice filled our comms. "Guys, that did something. Hold on."

A display popped up above my *sayar*, and I saw out of the corner of my eye that the same had happened with the other *sayars*. I watched the aliens for a reaction, nervous that they might have gotten spooked. If they noticed, they didn't show it. They waited, quietly rumbling.

"Whoa," I heard Fareedh say.

"Yeah," Marta said. "That makes sense."

"What?" I asked stupidly. Then I actually glanced down and saw what they were talking about. The display showed several views of the ball we'd transcribed, all of them snippets from the beginnings of lines. In addition to 'MATCH FOUND', they were now labeled with 'salutary greeting (hello)'.

"Guys!" I exclaimed. "It worked! We need to start naming things."

I looked excitedly at Marta, who looked amused, and Fareedh, who looked expectant. Pinky remained still. I guess he wanted to keep up the act for now. Well, that might be useful. I grabbed Fareedh and Marta by their arms and separated us from Pinky. Then I pointed to the three of us and said, "Human." I repeated the word, and Pinky gestured at us for emphasis, but kept quiet.

The beings didn't respond. Maybe I wasn't being clear enough. I fought down an instinct to speak loudly and slowly, like people sometimes do to Midworlders who don't speak French.

Marta took up the cause, pointing to us, repeating "human", then pausing and pointing to the beings. She added, "Alien."

This, they responded to. The leader, or at least the one who had guided us into the settlement and then, I think, was the one who had run his claws over Pinky's view pane, raised its arms, wiggled them at the other aliens, and chirped. Then it waved vaguely at us and made a different sound.

I looked down at the *sayar*, then frowned. Nothing.

"Not enough context," Marta said. "Hmmm."

She repeated her earlier performance, encompassing the three of us when she said, "Human." But this time, she pointed to both the group of beings and Pinky, and said, "Alien."

There was another peal of bird calls, abruptly silenced by a strong pulse of almost sub-sonic noise. Then the leader gestured to itself, and made a call. It waved its arms around to the group and made another call. Finally, it gestured to the four of us, the wave of its hand clearly including Pinky, and voiced a third sound.

"Those last two are what it said last time," Fareedh said. I couldn't tell. His ear was better than mine.

The alien wasn't done. Now it mirrored the gesture Marta had made, including its crowd with one sweep of its hand and pointing at Pinky with its other. It made a new sound, flat and mellow. The alien followed it up by pointing, specifically at the three of us this time, and shrilled, short with a sharp cut-off. I flinched; it sounded angry.

The *sayar* display blossomed. Several new words were labeled and glowing: "I/Me." "We/Us." "You (plural?)" "Alien/Other/Out-group/Stranger."

I felt a thrill. We could really learn their language!

"Let's repeat the sounds back to them, so they know we got it," Fareedh suggested.

"Already on it," Marta said. She gestured to the four of us and then had her *sayar* chirp out the word for "us".

The aliens all shuddered a little bit at the sound, suddenly agitated.

"That didn't go over well," I said.

"Hmm. I'm sure the pronunciation was right. Let me try another one." She stepped a pace from us, gestured to herself, and her *sayar* called out "I". She repeated it twice.

Again, they quivered, almost like a flinch. Each time, they turned their heads to the side. Then several of them raised their arms, waggling their second elbows in front of them, and calling forth a barrage of chirps we hadn't heard before.

"I think they want us to stop," Fareedh said.

"I don't understand," Marta said. "I'm sure we're saying it right. Could it mean something completely different when we say it? Is it contextual?"

I frowned. "I don't think it's what we're saying. They kind of looked like it hurt them when you talked with the *sayar*." I looked at Pinky, hoping he had some kind of insight, but he hadn't said a word since his utterance had upset the aliens.

"I wonder if it's our *sayars*," Fareedh ventured. "They don't have great fidelity." He'd complained about that before. The tiny built-in voicers were good enough, as far as I was concerned, but he always insisted on using room voicers instead.

"We could go back to the ship. Peter could make something, maybe."

"Maybe." Fareedh sounded doubtful.

That's when Pinky drew attention to himself for the first time. He stepped forward, then made an exact mimicry of what the alien had done, with a gesture to himself, then all of us. He chirped, twice, using the same words Marta had. The sound was different from what the *sayar* had produced, richer.

This time, the aliens didn't cringe. Their rumbles rose, and several stepped forward. The leader immediately called out "I" and "us", to which Pinky replied with exactly the same sounds and intonation.

Several of the aliens faced each other, clasping hands and purring like human-sized cats, obviously pleased.

That unlocked a one-way conversation, each of us finding as many things to name as possible. They never tried to repeat any of our words, French or otherwise. I don't think they were built for it. Nor did they have a *sayar*, or at least, not the kind we did, to keep up a running vocabulary.

But our list grew by leaps and bounds. We got through numbers quickly, plus basic physical objects, and the body parts we had in common. "Yes." "No." "Rock." "Butt." Two words for "elbow", one for each joint. Verbs that we could demonstrate, like "walk", "run", "sit", and so on. Things that we could see: their clothes, their shelters, the windscreen, even their spaceship. They had named it, so that had its own sound, but there was also a word it shared with *Majera*.

"It's not enough," Marta said, frustrated. "We've got dozens of words, but not enough to figure out a grammar. We need a way to get more."

We'd hit a wall. There's only so much you can demonstrate with gestures, so many objects whose purpose we both understood. When I tried showing them images from my *sayar* to broaden our vocabulary, they just rumbled at me in a way that I was beginning to recognize as a kind of question. The beings "saw" through echoes, not eyes. Those echoes were always being generated, too, and not just by the audible rumbles. Our *sayars* were constantly bombarded by pings across the spectrum. They couldn't see the holo displays, which had no physical substance.

"Oh, hold on," Fareedh said brightly. "Hey, Peter," he commed.

"Yeah?"

"Bring one of the newsballs to the airlock, would you? Then cycle the lock. I'll pick it up from there."

"Um, sure. Watch the wind, though. It's picking up again."

"Thanks."

With that, Fareedh ducked back out through the slit in the sheet. We all heard his "oof" over the comm as he disappeared. A moment later, he commed, "You weren't kidding about the wind, Peter."

I called out, "You going to be alright?"

"Oh sure."

Peter chided, "If you weren't skin and bones…"

"Less wind resistance," Fareedh replied. There was a smile to it, but it was also clear he was exerting himself.

I turned back to the aliens and twiddled my fingers for a long moment. "I wish we could tell them what's going on."

Pinky gave me an "OK" sign, then chirped some sounds. My *sayar* translated <Stop> and <Little>. The alien leader called back: <Yes>. I felt a glow of connection. And pride. We were *talking* to aliens. Real, live aliens. *We* were.

A little bit of acid crept up from my stomach. Lord, don't let us somehow screw up this first contact.

The aliens were good at standing still, but I wasn't. I shuffled my feet, and vaguely realized I would have to pee eventually. I decided it wasn't urgent. That led to the funny thought of all of us ducking out in the middle of this, one by one, to go to the bathroom on the ship.

At last, Fareedh returned, lurching through the screen with dust showering off his bubble helmet.

"Whew," he gasped. "That was something. Anyway, I've got it. Them, actually. Peter gave me the ball with the solar system map, too."

He was clutching a fuzzy ball in each of his gloved hands. The intensity of the beings' rumbles and pings rose as they scanned him. I wondered if they could read the balls all the way from there.

"I wish we could tell them they've been decontaminated," Marta said worriedly.

"Let Pinky hold one," I suggested.

Fareedh handed the ball in his right hand to him. "Good idea. I think this is the space ball."

So now Pinky stood there, awkwardly, like a statue of an alien with a ball in his outstretched claw.

"What was your idea?" I asked. "The maps and stuff?"

Fareedh's nod was dimly visible in his helmet glow. "They're the only pictures we know they can see."

With the newsball in his left hand and his *sayar* stuck to his belt, he ran his right index finger over the alien newsball. Images whizzed past in a pair of displays floating above him. Wherever his fingertip pressed, the *sayar's* display showed an enormously expanded view of what he was touching, as well as the "transcript" of wavy audio bands. I linked my *sayar* with his so my displays mirrored them. Eventually, he got to the solar system map.

No reaction from the beings.

"Get closer," Marta urged.

"Sure," Fareedh said absently. He and Pinky shuffled toward the beings. The leader approached them, and they paused, maybe two meters apart. Suddenly, it exclaimed, a whole sentence of tweets and caws. It faced Pinky, not Fareedh, and plucked the newsball from his left hand. It caressed it almost lovingly, continuing its monologue. The others came forward, one at a time at first, then in a rush, until they were huddled together around the leader in front of Fareedh. They were all chattering now, their voices somehow intense without being loud.

Then the quality of their sounds changed, became almost a unified keening, to where I couldn't make out words, nor could the ship's *sayar*. The leader clutched the ball, and its claw seemed to shake with the strength of its grip. The others, all of them, knelt suddenly to the ground, almost as if in a faint. Their wails rose, the differences flattening between them until there was just a single note — penetrating and plaintive. I felt my teeth rattle with it.

"What are… are they crying?" I whispered. "Lord. They didn't know." I felt the sting come to my eyes. We'd brought the balls just to get their word for "planet"; instead we'd given them the news of their race's death. I felt like a jerk.

At last, the leader, if that's what it was, raised its hands up, and the mournful sounds slowly faded. It walked up to Pinky, placing its free claw gently on his shoulder. It chirped, and my *sayar* translated, <FIRST CONTINENT-DWELLER>. I blinked. They hadn't used the word before; the ship's *sayar* must have correlated it with something on the newsball or maybe a building.

Pinky called back in their sounds: <No>.

The being stiffened slowly. I saw that it was half a head taller than Pinky, even with him trying to mimic the alien form.

It called, more intensely. The *sayar* paused, then translated: <SECOND CONTINENT-DWELLER>.

My breath caught.

<No>, Pinky replied.

With that, Pinky began to change. The leader sprang back as if stung, then rumbled like an earth mover as my friend sprouted a third leg and shortened a good half-meter, rounding up around the middle.

When he was done, Pinky chirped, <I>.

More softly, and clearly relieved, he muttered in French, "That's *much* better."

The alien, to its credit, seemed to take things in stride. It gave the ball back to Pinky, then waited patiently. Fareedh coughed, then put his hand back on its fuzzy surface, searching until he'd found the diagram again.

<Yes,> the being said, and it placed a pair of claws on Fareedh's gloved hand, guiding his finger slowly along. The alien chirped a litany of separate words as the yellow highlighting glow flitted across the system diagram in Fareedh's display. The being repeated the act, exactly, from the start.

Our *sayars* popped up a dozen new words, from "space" to "planet" to "orbit". My heart began to race. Now the alien held up the newsball and guided Fareedh's finger quickly to the world maps. More words flowed into the lexicon: "Ocean." "River." "Water."

A pause. Fareedh's fingertip was on the tower of dots next to the first city we'd landed in. "Death," it said.

None of us made a sound.

The being went methodically over the entire ball, calling out chirps in an untiring torrent. New words cascaded down the display lists. It methodically went through diagram after diagram, more than I'd remembered having been on the artifact, and always that staccato stream of sounds. It must have been clarifying, defining as it went: whole columns of words sprang up next to the noun list: prepositions; conjunctions; verbs. When it was done, it went back to the space ball and repeated the performance with its four diagrams.

And waited.

I swallowed on a dry throat, realizing my lips had been parted the whole time, and glanced down at my other display, the one with the transcripted text bands.

Virtually every single word was labeled.

The quiet moment stretched, the four of us looking at each other, none of us sure what to do next. Then I put a hand on Pinky's shoulder and handed him my *sayar*.

"Can you tell them who we are?"

"Rodger dodger, Captain." What I could see of his skin through his view pane was an excited hot pink, clearly visible even in the diffuse light of the displays.

Pinky drew himself up, arms stretched like a stage performer, and sounds began to issue forth, their French translation popping up as free-floating words in the air above him.

<We are aliens from the stars. We are also your friends. We came in our spaceship from [ALIEN NAME FOR PLANET #2]. We came to help.>

The beings were frozen, as if stunned. Then they repeated their earlier display, clutching hands and each other, rumbling and moaning...but not for long. Two of them broke from the group and came toward us at a trot. Before I knew it, the whole crowd was rushing toward us. I flinched and braced instinctively to run, but they were upon us before I could move, hemming us in, their probing sounds making my teeth vibrate, their strange-jointed arms wrapped around us. Had we upset them? Were they going to hurt us?

Then I saw the translation, filling the air in the gaps between alien bodies.

<Thank you thank you thank you thank you thank you…>

Chapter Thirteen

There had been two intelligent races of beings on Pesadumbre. Both sides had started out as dozens of countries, but within the last couple of generations—however long that was for them, we still weren't sure—they had consolidated into superpowers, each filling a continent. So the story went, the round-headed people of the first continent were noble, kind, industrious. The square-headed beings of the second continent were malicious and venal. The wars had gone on for decades, with sporadic periods of tense armistice. The last pause had gone on for eleven of their years, and it seemed that a real breakthrough in peace talks might be possible. In this hopeful pause, the first continent sent out an expedition to Planet One, for science.. and as a hedge against disaster.

Then the sky fell.

A surgical strike began the orbital war. In no time, most of the satellites were gone, disrupting communications and blinding each side to what was happening on each other's continent. Somehow, both sides held back their strongest weapons: long-ranged missiles tipped with nuclear warheads. The round-headed aliens did so out of a spirit of peaceful caution. The square-heads because they had something more sinister in mind.

That's when the plague broke out, seemingly everywhere at once. It happened too fast for a coordinated response. Some groups made it to shelter, like the ones we'd found in that first city. Others, maybe the majority, had died in the streets.

But the square-heads had somehow gotten caught in their own trap. Whatever they'd unleashed on the first continent had spread like wildfire in their own country. Obviously, the two races had a close common ancestor; whatever deadly concoction the square-heads had whipped up, it affected them no less strongly. The result was a dead planet.

At least, that was the story we got, pieced together from the sources we had: the news ball, conversations with the Pesadumbrans, and what we'd found on their homeworld. There was really no way to confirm if the square-heads were really the nefarious thugs the newsball made them out to be, or if they had come up with the doomsday virus or gas or whatever. There wasn't anyone left to dispute the official story, or at least, the one reported in the single edition of the news that got out before it was all over.

The survivors on Planet One had been completely in the dark, denied even that bit of news. As far as they'd known, their homeworld had simply stopped talking to them. They'd feared the worst, but they'd held hopes that maybe beings still lived on their home planet. We'd dashed them.

Now the mess was in our laps.

"We could go to the second continent again," Peter suggested. "To verify the story." He leaned back in his chair, swiveling to rest an elbow on the wardroom table. I kicked myself mentally again for having left the fuzzy cube back in the robot city. On the other hand, it might not have told us much. It might have just been full of office memos.

Fareedh spread out a dubious hand. "I don't need to get shot at. Again. Anyway, we're in a hurry, right?"

I nodded. "There are thirty-two Pesadumbrans left in the universe, so far as we know. I don't want to come back and find any fewer." With a sigh, I added, "I just wish we could take them back home with us."

"I don't mind offering up my room," Pinky said. "I can sleep up there with Jub-Jub." He made a show of squaring off his head to match the contours of the creature's enclosure. Only momentarily, though. Pinky hates sharp corners.

Marta giggled. "That's nice of you, but even if we had the space, we couldn't risk it. Just bringing them in contact with our suits, even after we sterilized them, was a risk. Plus, we don't know what effect we might have on them, or vice versa."

"And," Fareedh noted wryly, "if we get back during Dust season, they'll just wish they were back home."

I smiled at that, and after a moment, I snorted softly, looking down at the matte expanse of the table.

"What's funny, Kitra?" Pinky asked.

I looked up at him. "For the first time, we have an easy decision. There's nothing more we can do. We just have to go home and hope the government can help them." I frowned, dissatisfied. "I just hope they didn't expect more from us."

Pinky put a comforting paw on my shoulder. "I'll tell them. I'm sure it'll be fine. All we can do is all we can do."

I shook my head. "I think we all should talk to them."

Who knew if we'd ever see them again?

It was daylight, and the dust storm had abated, leaving a harsh cyan sky. The ramshackle nature of the alien settlement was more obvious in the glare of the oversized sun. Circular dwellings were made of native stone and panels of shiny metal or plastic, fused together without much concern for artistry. The bumpy, gleaming spaceship in the center of the colony looked intact, but I suspected the inside had been hollowed out for materials. The Pesadumbrans had lowered the barrier that had ringed their little village, allowing the dry breeze to keep the area from getting intolerably hot.

Two of the aliens stood before us, wrapped in tattered, colorless shawls. They might have been the same ones who had spoken for the group before, but I couldn't tell for sure. The rest of the exiles milled about restless behind them. They'd come out of their homes or dropped their farm and maintenance tools to meet us when we'd arrived. All five of us had come. No one wanted to stay behind. How could I blame them?

"It is time for us to go," I said. "But we will make sure you are helped." Pinky, three hands on his hips, swelled slightly and repeated my words in their language.

The leftward one of the alien pair chirped, my *sayar* translating: <Can you take us back home?>

I shook my head, then remembered that the gesture would be meaningless to them. "We cannot. What killed your people back there might still linger."

<We can not go home?> The alien waved its thin arms in what looked like agitation.

Marta spoke up, "We don't know that. We can find out, in time."

<How long?> The question came from the other one of the pair.

"How long… you mean how long until we can find out?"

<Yes.>

Marta spread her arms out in a shrug. "We will have to go to our home and notify our leaders. They will send experts to your world and get more knowledge." She was careful to use words she knew had been translated already.

<It will be years.> the rightward one said.

"No," Peter cut in. "Our ships are very fast."

<Are your leaders as fast?>

"They can be," I said. I couldn't imagine them sitting on this, only the fourth time the Empire had made first contact.

Fareedh added, "For now, this place isn't working out too badly for you."

Silence stretched. There was a hiss as swirling dust caught on a breeze was strewn across the ground and the transparent field covers.

Then, one of the aliens lurched forward a step from the crowd. It looked different from the others, with a bulged mid-section puffing out its sheath-like clothes. It also carried a small bundle in its arms.

<Please. Take this child. We will all die here. At least give this one a chance for life.>

As I watched, the bundle moved slightly and let out a high pitched warble that buzzed my ear drums.

"We can't," Marta said. "You see we are protecting ourselves with clothing. We don't know what will happen if our people are exposed to your people directly."

<You are afraid of us?> another called out from the crowd.

Fareedh answered, "No. We are afraid for you. You have worked so hard to survive. We cannot take the chance of losing even one of your people."

"But we will do everything we can," Marta interjected, "As quickly as we can."

Silence again, for the most part. I was aware of a subsonic rumble. Some of them must have been talking, perhaps in their equivalent of a murmur.

The rightward of the pair in front of us let out a single, flat note. The rumble stopped. Then the alien began chirping again.

<They have come as friends,> the *sayar* translated. <I believe they will do their best.>

"We will," I said. "That's a promise."

A pause. Then the two representatives chirped in unison. It was translated:

<The oath is made.>

I swallowed, looking nervously from the pair to the ragged group behind them, all stock still like the statue we had seen in the plaza of that doomed city. So long ago, it seemed now.

Then I ventured a smile, even knowing it wouldn't mean anything to them.

"Yes," I said. "An oath is made."

Launch +46

I woke myself up the first back night in hyperspace with a small cry, my heart racing. Shards of dream flew from my mind in the sharp transition leaving one overriding image blazing in my consciousness: an armada of green ships surrounding *Majera* menacingly before rushing in.

The sheets were damp with sweat. I sat up, the room lights coming to quarter intensity. The sight of familiar things already began banishing the nightmare image with their humdrum solidity: The Cleaner, transparent and ceiling height in the corner; the holo of Helmi on the ruins of Talvi, my *sayar*, even the dirty laundry strewn across the floor. I took deep breaths and deliberately turned my gaze to the Exhibit Table for more distraction. The sight of the matching fossil shells from Hyvilma, twin gifts from Fareedh and Marta, nestled between the salt shaker Pinky had filched from the *Faucon* and the coaster from *Le Frontiére*, made me smile.

The smile faded as my eyes slid over the newest addition to my exhibit: the doll from the second continent. Dream fears and phantoms, instead of disappearing, merged with more grounded concerns, and fresh sweat prickled as I had a sudden, chilling notion about what had really happened to the Pesadumbrans.

I snatched a look at the *sayar*. It was around 5 AM, ship's time. Too late to go back to sleep, which seemed out of the question anyway. My head buzzed with the rag end of thoughts, all marinating in a sense of foreboding.

I needed coffee. I got up, threw on a shirt and shorts, and opened the door, figuring no one would be up so early.

I was wrong. Pinky was there in the wardroom, and Jub-Jub was out of its cage and crouched on the table. It looked like they were playing tug of war with a painting stylus. Pinky rolled his eyespots toward me and rumbled out a "Good morning" without taking a break in his struggle. I watched, fascinated as Pinky's arm stretched out, Jub-Jub drawing the stylus closer to its mandibles. Pinky didn't strain back as a human might; he just retracted his appendages until they were almost flush with his body. At last, he simply absorbed the stylus into himself, where it remained dimly visible under his skin. Jub-Jub scratched futilely at it.

"That's not really fair," I said. "It's also gross. You didn't use sleight of hand this time."

Pinky flushed a deeper red, which I would have taken for a blush if I hadn't known him better, and if he hadn't giggled. He extruded the stylus with a "ptui!" sound and let the little creature have it.

"Is it safe for it to have that thing?" I asked. Pinky grew back his arm just so he could shrug.

But instead of gnawing on the stylus, like I thought it would, Jub-Jub was waving the tool around like a dueling epee. It seemed to be enjoying itself. I revised my estimate of its intelligence up once again.

"What are you doing awake, anyway?" Pinky asked.

"Coffee," I mumbled, heading toward the galley. For a moment, I considered letting the Maker produce its usual, mediocre brew. It'd be quick and easy. But no, I'd had enough of that junk to last a lifetime. I was going to do it right.

"Pinky, I had a scary thought," I said, washing out my *cezve* and then filling it up with a cup of water.

"Peter in balloon pants?"

I barked out a laugh. "Not *that* scary." Where had I put the coffee? Ah, there it was. Someone had put a bag of flour in front of it. I opened up the grinder and eyed it. Clean enough.

"No," I went on, "I was thinking. The plague, or whatever it *was*, got everyone at once. I could see that happening on one continent, if it was delivered with missiles, but it happened to *both*, simultaneously."

Pinky's response was drowned out by the grinder. "What did you say?" I asked when I'd finished.

"I said, we don't know that it happened at the same time. Maybe the second continent got it a couple of weeks later from a rogue wind or something."

I spooned the coffee into the *cezve* and put it on the hot plate. It would take a minute to warm up, so I turned around. Pinky's arms were folded in his three-legged lap. Jub-Jub had put down the stylus and was looking at me attentively.

"They'd have been better prepared, then, and it wouldn't have hit all of them at once. Like when we get a pollen storm, it hits Denizli before it gets to Mersin, and sometimes it misses Tokat entirely."

He spread out his hands in a very human gesture. Jub-Jub mirrored it. My lips quirked at the sight.

"So," Pinky said, "What was the vector?"

"I think it had to come from space."

"Delivered by satellite?" he asked.

I nodded. "That was my first thought. The square-heads started dropping poison bombs, the round-heads tried blowing up their satellites. A big battle took place in orbit, and then some of the satellites crashed into the second continent."

Pinky pulsed purple. "That's reasonable. And scary alright."

I swallowed. "That's not actually the scary bit."

"Oh?"

I took a deep breath, not sure I wanted to give life to my fears. Then I plunged in. "What if it wasn't the square-heads at all?"

"You think our friends might have done it?"

I shook my head and opened my mouth to answer, but a hiss behind me interrupted my thinking. I took a second to scoop off the froth and put it into my cup. When I was certain the coffee was simmering but not boiling, I turned back around.

"I'm wondering if it was something, you know, alien."

Pinky shaded a hideous ochre. "Surely, you're not blaming *Jub-*

Jub!"

"I'm serious!"

He quickly turned pink again. "I'm sorry. Go on."

"What if it was, I don't know, a meteor with some strange disease on it. Or…and this is what really scares me…what if there's some race out there that poisoned the planet deliberately?" A green flotilla blazed in my mind's eye.

Pinky got up and wrapped his pseudopods around me, his eyespots level with my chest, looking up at me.

"That sounds terrible. I don't want to believe it."

I shivered at the thought, the idea that any being could willingly commit genocide like that. Pinky squeezed me a little tighter.

"Yeah."

"But, we don't know," he said. "And anyway, your first idea makes more sense. What is it your mother always said?"

I smiled. "Don't borrow trouble."

"Yeah."

I pet him on his nubbin noggin. "You're the best."

"I know."

A soft *clunk* marked the opening of the door to Marta and Peter's room, and Pinky let me go. Marta padded in, uncharacteristically disheveled. She had slept in her and Peter's room the night before, leaving me alone and a little lonely. My heart jumped a bit, the way it used to when we had first started going out. Marta yawned a good morning, then tilted her chin up, sniffing like a cat.

"Are you making coffee?"

"Yeah. Did you want some?"

"Please!"

I turned to measure out some more foam from the gently bubbling pot into a cup for her. She came over and slid her arms around me from behind. She was very warm, and my eyes fluttered closed. She smelled like cinnamon and figs; I loved it when she used that soap.

"I cannot wait to get home," she said groggily.

"Me too," I said with a sigh. "Lord, there's so much to do, between the aliens and the patents and the…"

"I just mean *home*," she cut in. I thought I heard a little tremble in her voice. "Free air we can breathe without suits. A real bath. A break from... Well, a time to regroup, you know?" She squeezed more tightly, desperately.

I rested my palms on her encircling arms. "I'm sorry. Yeah. I'm sure we can all use that." My hands found hers, and slowly, her hug softened against my chest. We'd all been left a bit scarred. Some of the scars, like Fareedh's, were literal. Marta's hurt, on the other hand, was further down. We hadn't talked about it since the robots. When we got back, we couldn't just take care of chores. We had to take care of ourselves, too. That couldn't even start until we'd had some time off the ship, I realized.

"Hey, Kitra," Marta was saying. "What if you moved out of your Uncle's place?"

A spitting sound in front of me made me jump. My eyes sprang open, just in time to get spattered with spray from popping bubbles. I turned down the heat. The coffee was pretty much done. I poured some into Marta's cup, then mine. Not as much as I'd planned; I hadn't expected to be brewing for two. Marta let go to look for the sugar. On an impulse, I looked over my shoulder.

Pinky had left at some point, and he'd put Jub-Jub back in its enclosure. Maybe he'd gone to give us some space, or maybe he'd just gotten tired of watching us hug.

I looked back at Marta, swallowed, and said. "You mean move in with you?"

She stirred, met my eye, and nodded. "I was thinking," she said softly, "how nice it could be."

"How do you mean?"

"Well...we get back home, and we have to stay put for a bit. Infinity knows we've packed enough into this last year. And then we, you know, file our reports, Peter turns in his research, works on his patents." She put her coffee down and gave my arm a little squeeze. "Imagine a private space bigger than three meters square," Marta murmured.

Now my heart was thudding. "Just you and me?"

"Well... you and me and the others."

My reaction must have been obvious.

"Hey, what's wrong?" she asked, a wrinkle appearing between

her eyebrows.

I looked down. "I guess I just. I dunno. Fareedh did say…but…" My right thumb sought out fingertips and began sliding back and forth. "I don't know if I want to share. Not like that."

Marta tilted my chin up. Her eyes were shining, shimmering green.

"You're not sharing. You have 100% of my love, always."

I shook my head. "But there's Peter. And now Fareedh. How? I mean, mathematically? How do you divide 100 three ways and get 100? How can that work?"

She shrugged her soft shoulders. "I don't know. It just does. I *love* you, Kitra. I want you in my life so badly. I always have."

My eyes darted from hers: to the seat Pinky had vacated, to Jub-Jub, curled up quietly in its enclosure, to the cabinets along the other wall.

She took my hand in both of hers, pressed it to her cheek.

"Why can't you look at me?" she asked, a quaver in her voice.

I did, then. Tears had begun snaking their way down her freckled cheeks. She was blindingly, perfectly beautiful.

"Because you're too much," I said softly. And then, so I couldn't be misinterpreted, I stood on my tiptoes, cupped her cheeks, and kissed her. She returned the kiss fiercely, and for a moment, it was just me and her, our arms around each other, and the rest of the universe didn't exist.

Then I gently pressed her shoulders, making space between us. "I want to be with you Marta," I said. "As much as anything." I looked up at her.

"But?" she asked, anxious.

"I just need to think about how to make it work."

"I…" she paused, then shook her head, brown ringlets bobbing. "No, I'll shut up. You think."

I smiled sheepishly and took a sip of coffee. I'd waited too long. It hardly scalded my tongue at all. Oh well. It still tasted good.

"You want me to leave you be?" she asked.

That was a hard question to answer. Part of me wanted to take Marta to my stateroom and cuddle with her until *Majera* got home. But there was too much roiling in my head.

"Just for a little bit," I said.

She nodded solemnly and gave me a kiss on the forehead, then took her coffee and went quietly back into her room, leaving me alone in the wardroom. I took another sip of my tepid brew, a pleasant bitter tingle on my tongue. Then, on a sudden impulse, I walked beside the wardroom table and through the door onto the bridge.

Pinky was there, standing two-legged and three-armed in the open space behind our seats, between Peter and Fareedh's stations. He stared at a display in the Window, a three-dimensional star chart. The scale was quickly obvious from the river of starless void that ran through the middle of it: the Rift. The golden sun of Hyvilma glowed on one side, little red Punainen on the other. Thin lines wove a pattern that extended from Pesudumbre's star all the way back to the orange and red pair that marked the Vatan system — a record of all of our journeys, I quickly realized, from our first Jump to Jaiyk to now.

Without turning or rotating his spots, he asked, "Are you glad to be going home?"

"That's a good question," I said. I added a little too quickly, "Are you?"

His skin shaded faintly chartreuse. "I was kind of getting used to the idea of *Majera* as home."

I chuckled. "Yeah, I see what you mean."

Now he did turn, completely, not just his eyespots. "Do you really?"

"Well, we have been on the ship more than we've been off it for a while now." I frowned slightly. "But that's not what you mean, is it?"

"No."

"Don't you miss, you know, being back on Vatan?"

"What's waiting for me back there?"

"Your whole family, right?"

He flushed maroon with seeming puzzlement. "*You're* my family."

I tried again, "I mean, you know, all of...of your kind." It struck me that I'd known Pinky for half of my life, and I still didn't know what they called themselves.

Stiffly, he replied, "As I said, you guys are my kind."

Something in his tone stopped me short. "Pinky, are you mad at me for something?"

His skin slowly faded back to its normal pink, and he made a good approximation of that clicking sound Fareedh made, tongue against teeth, when he meant "no." Then he came toward me, his eye-spots boring up into my eyes.

"Kitra," he began, his voice soft and thin, "I'm a big phoney."

"What?" I said, surprised.

"I play at being people. I thought if I was people enough, I wouldn't have to worry about this happening. But I'm not people. I'm just me. I'm not even sure what me is these days. So now I'm going to lose you."

Sweat clammed my skin, and my stomach flopped. "Why in space would you believe that?"

"I have eyes, Kitra." His spots parted disconcertingly for a moment before narrowing again. "Well, eyespots, anyway." He seemed to sag a little. "And I guess that's the problem."

"I still don't understand," I said, though it wasn't quite true.

He paused. I didn't know if he was thinking or waiting. Before I could answer, he was talking again. "It's different with my kind. We don't... there's no boundary between 'me' and 'we'. When we're together, it all sort of blends.

"Going to the human school, I had to learn how to be my own 'me'. It was so much work, but I had to do it, because I wanted to learn how to be a 'we' with people. The closest I got was with you. You and me, Kitra. We're a 'we', and when I'm with you, I feel like 'me'."

I blinked rapidly, clearing my eyes. I guess I'd always taken Pinky's...humanity...for granted. Sure, he was a featureless shapechanger, but I'd thought that inside, his soul was basically like mine. Like anyone's. When he'd let glimpses of his alien nature peep out to the surface, it had scared me. It felt like I was losing him.

Maybe I'd really been seeing him for the first time.

"You're my best friend," I said.

"Yes, that's the phrase. Best friends. That's our 'we'." He cocked his head to the side in a very human gesture. "It's more complicated now, though. I love the others, too, even if Marta smells funny and Fareedh's corners are too sharp and Peter can't dance. We are all best friends. And now it's going to end."

"Of course not! I'm sure we'll fly again."

"I'm not just talking about *Majera*. Though, honestly, I'm happier in my little stateroom than I ever was at the dormitories. Or at the Creche."

I hadn't heard him talk about the Creche in a long time. I dimly remembered a blue dome at one end of the circular compound that his people lived in on Vatan.

"But I thought we were forming a..." he seemed to stumble for words, "a unit. A family." His voice went flat. "I didn't realize I hadn't been invited."

"You mean...me and Marta."

"And the others. I'm sorry. I couldn't help hearing. And seeing. It's obvious, even to me. When we get back to Vatan, all this is over. This new 'we' is over."

I opened my mouth to respond, but found the words wouldn't come.

A pause. Then Pinky added, "You and the others are people. I'm not a people."

I flinched as if he'd slapped me. And I was suddenly angry. Not at him, but at me. At us. "You *are* people. And you *are* family. Don't ever say you're not."

"But you're going to make a unit with Marta and the others."

I put my hands on two of his shoulders and looked down at him. "Okay, firstly, I haven't made that decision. And secondly, why does it matter? It didn't bother you when Marta and I were going out before."

"That was different."

"Why?"

"I didn't know better."

I blinked.

"I've been studying, and I've learned a bit from L'Eclair. About 'relationships'." The way he said it, I could hear the quotes. "It's going to be all of you, my closest friends, and the circle will be closed. Where is the room for me? How can there be? A relationship is for people."

My eyes started to sting. I straightened and gripped his shoulders tightly.

"Well, maybe it's time to expand the definition." I went on more firmly. "Because whatever we do, whatever I decide, there's no way you're going to stop being the most important *person* in the universe to me."

Pinky eyed me impassively. "But what about the others?"

I felt my jaw set. "Obviously, I need to get everybody together and talk to them about it. Right now. Either they're okay with it or they're not, but you and me," I gestured at my chest and his, "we're forever."

His color deepened slowly. "You mean that?" he said in a small voice.

I nodded. "Roger Dodger."

He crushed me in a hug, which is really something when three arms are involved.

Chapter Fourteen

After almost seven weeks of travel, the starboard cargo bay was near-ly empty, which made it a nice, spacious place to meet. There were still a few pallets of supplies: the different varieties of Maker goop and the stasised and preserved foods that the Maker can't get quite right. My coffee, for instance. Peter's lingonberry jam. But it was better than the larboard bay, which was packed with the bigger pieces of spare equipment that wouldn't fit in the workshop—that myriad of stuff you inventory just in case something goes *pffft* in space. Also the junk Peter was storing on board for his various projects. He still hadn't quite explained which was hobby stuff and which was essential. It wouldn't really matter until we needed the space for the air car we planned to buy.

I frowned, remembering that it might be a very long time before our next flight.

"You okay, Kitra?" Pinky asked. He was carrying a triple-armload of cushions he'd gotten from his room, and he had to peer around them to see me, eyespots on an extended serpent of a head.

"Yeah, just thinking," I said. I put my own porta-seat next to a box of circuit goop, inflated it, and plopped down. Pinky began pacing around the room, making considering noises. He placed a cushion, then moved it around with a foot, fussing with its exact placement until he was satisfied. Then he went on to the next one.

I watched, suppressing a bemused smile. We'd been through more in the last year than most experienced in a lifetime, and most of those events still hadn't finished playing out. There was an entire alien race to save, maybe a planet to decontaminate. This new drive Peter had invented might change the way travel worked across the galaxy.

Not to mention we were still waiting for another boot to drop after the insurrection at Hyvilma and Sennet. And here we were, camped out in a storage hangar, organizing seats to resolve who was going to be dating whom — and who wasn't going to be left out. It all seemed kind of ridiculous. What were our petty issues compared to all of the bigger crises we'd gotten mixed up in?

I shook my head with a violent little shiver. No, Marta had been right when she'd said on Hyvilma that nothing was more important than family. Our own crisis was just as valid as any other. And, I thought, letting my smile grow, it's not like we could solve any of our other problems while we were stuck in hyperspace. Might as well fix what we could.

At last, Pinky seemed satisfied. He surveyed his circle of seats, two arms crooked, massive fists resting on the sides of the round swell above his legs, a third arcing in front of him, looking for all the universe like a teapot handle.

He said, "That's a proper circle, I think."

"Shall I comm the others?" I rapped my *sayar* against the goop box meaningfully. There was a hollow *thunk*; the box was empty.

"Ready when you are," he said.

The ring of seats Pinky'd put together had us all maybe a meter and a half apart. Marta sat across from me, looking over my shoulder and said, "You know, I think the room would look more homey with color, maybe brown? Kitra, like the inside of the old-style ships in your stories."

I swiveled to look at the bare gray walls, vaguely pearlescent in the bright light from the ceiling panels, before turning back to shrug.

Fareedh, to her left, was nodding, "Yeah. We could put up a wall-to-wall sprawl with wood grain." He put his thumb to his lip contemplatively. "Or maybe a Julia fractal. It could curl up from that corner to that one," he said, the sleeve of his tunic sliding to his elbow as he gestured.

Marta wrinkled her nose. "I dunno. Hyperspace is weird enough. I was thinking something more grounded."

Peter, sitting on my right, scoffed, "Guys, it's a cargo hold," echoing my thoughts. He looked over at me, leaning forward on his cushion as he braced his hands on his knees. "Why are we meeting in here, anyway?"

I smiled sheepishly, placing my palms flat on the deck; my fingers were itching to slide nervously against each other. "It seemed like a change of scenery was a good idea. We might as well make use of the space now that we've got it." I looked down at a seam in the green cushion Peter was squishing almost to the floor with his bulk. "There's a lot to talk about."

"Yeah there is," Peter said emphatically. "I haven't even begun figuring out how I'm going to present my findings. I've got the math worked out, but when I try to establish a context, all my drafts end up reading like an adventure script, not a journal paper."

"Maybe you should pitch it to *Yeşilçam*?" Fareedh teased.

"I didn't say it was a *good* script…"

Marta edged in gently, "Guys, I don't think that's what Kitra is talking about."

"Oh right," Fareedh said. He settled down and looked at me expectantly with deep brown eyes

I cleared my throat. "Yeah, so, I know there's a lot going on. But we've got a calm before the storm, so to speak, and I wanted to work things out before we got home. Between us, I mean." I swallowed, then plunged on, "Both of you," I said, nodding to Marta and Fareedh, "have given me an invitation, and now that I know the shape of things, I've been thinking about it."

They were all quiet. Pinky's expression was blank as usual, Peter looked a bit anxious, Marta smiled encouragingly.

"This is a big deal," I said. "I mean, it changes everything." I was stalling, still not sure how I felt. No, I knew how I *felt*, just not what to do about it.

Fareedh waved a hand casually. "It doesn't have to change much. It's still just us."

"Sure, but, I hadn't thought of 'us' as *us*, you know? Not like that. I mean… well… for instance," I looked over at Peter, "I mean, how do you feel about me just crashing your party? You've got history with Marta, and Fareedh…" I trailed off, hoping he'd pick up my train of thoughts. Maybe offer me an exit. Not because I necessarily wanted one, but because it seemed easier than having to figure all of this out, and maybe hurt anyone else.

He looked at me seriously, then blurted. "Kitra, I've been in love with you ever since the Émilie."

"Wait, what?!" Marta and I both exclaimed at the same time.

Fareedh chuckled. "It wasn't obvious?"

Marta said to Peter, "That long? I knew you were okay with inviting Kitra in, but…I didn't realize…"

I looked at Peter, eyes wide. He was staring at the deck, his face flushed almost as pink as Pinky. Out of all the unexpected things that had happened in the last year, this won the prize. Before we'd flown together, Peter, at best, had tolerated me. That's how it had felt, anyway. Sure, we'd been friends, but we were always teasing each other, and he seemed a bit disdainful, even resentful of me, even though *he* was the one going out with Marta. And, yeah, things had changed recently, but…in love with *me*? With Fareedh, I could see. Or at least, I was getting used to the idea. *I* liked Fareedh. But I just didn't see

Peter that way. Maybe that's why I couldn't imagine him seeing me that way.

On the other hand, there's nothing to make you reconsider all of your preconceived notions like a confession.

Marta looked worriedly at Peter, then me. "I'm sorry," she said. "We don't want to scare you off." Peter flushed further at that and looked positively miserable.

I wasn't scared off. It certainly was a lot to take in, but knowing they *all* had feelings for me actually seemed to make things simpler. This way, there were no toes to step on.

I felt a frown form on my face. Was it really simpler? If I jumped into…whatever it was they were contemplating, they might want more from me than I could give. I felt my heart race faster, and I had the instinct to flee — to the bridge, my room, even out the airlock into hyperspace nothingness.

I fought it down and held up a pausing palm. If I could just get on solid ground…

"Okay. First," I said. Then I realized I felt starved for air. My breath rushed in, filling my chest until my lungs seemed to click against my sternum. I let it out slowly and turned to Peter.

"First," I repeated, "Thank you." He looked up at me, stunned. "Really. You're very brave to say something like that right out." My voice softened. "It means a lot." It felt like I was channeling Marta; I don't think I would have had those words a year before.

He tried to smile. "It was stupid. It just came right out. I haven't told anyone."

I shook my head. "No, it's great," I said, then chuckled, surprised. "I really mean that."

"But?" Fareedh prompted.

"Well, it's not so much a 'but'. I just need to get some things straight. I know I'm in love with Marta," Marta smiled softly at that, her eyes shining, "and I came into this figuring maybe it'd be me and her as sort of its own thing, but tied in with everything else. Some-how. Now I'm wrestling with the idea that maybe that's not how you all think this thing would work." I flapped my hands uselessly. "And maybe I'm not against whatever your feeling about 'us' is." I sighed. "It's not that I'm clueless about these kinds of things, really."

Fareedh laughed. "Yes you are."

I flushed through a smile. "Okay, maybe I am. I'm bad enough one on one. But one on three? Or whatever?"

Marta's forehead creased, and she reached across the circle for my hand. I stretched out and let her take it.

"This can be whatever you want it to be, Kitra." Her voice cracked slightly.

I gripped her hand tightly, feeling like I was about to melt. Her fingers trembled, and her eyes darted slightly left and right, reading my expression.

A little nod, and then a swallow. "I think I'm willing to try," I found myself saying. "With all of you. But..."

Fareedh leaned forward from his usual slouch and watched me.

"This really is a 'but'." I looked over at Pinky, who hadn't uttered a peep or even moved. His color was neutral, too. He might as well have been a pink, half-melted statue of a man.

Turning back to the rest, I said, "Whatever we do, it can't exclude Pinky."

Peter coughed on a swallow. When he'd recovered, he managed weakly, "How's that again?"

"Just what I said," I replied. "If we're going to be something, together, however that shakes out, Pinky can't be left on the outside."

I looked over at my best friend again. His eyespots had rolled over to meet my gaze. "He's one of us," I finished. He pulsed slightly at that, and he dipped his head almost imperceptibly.

"What do you say to that?" I looked back at them, one to the next.

Fareedh broke into a grin. "Kitra, I've been in love with Pinky ever since the Émilie," wryly mimicking Peter's words.

Peter thumped Fareedh on the shoulder at the same time Marta exclaimed, "That's not funny, Fareedh!"

Fareedh spread his hands, "Hey, who's kidding?"

In the middle of the uproar, Pinky made a dramatic throat-clearing sound. Things settled down immediately.

"You don't have to make a big deal on my account," he said in his smoothest, holo-star baritone. "I'm happy for all of you, really. Obviously, this has been a long time coming, and who can blame you? You're all the best people I know. It's only natural you should want to form a bond together. Please don't worry about me," he said with pitch-perfect sincerity. He began to take to his feet.

"Now look," Fareedh said, surprisingly angry. "Granted, the tone was flip, but I mean it." His voice softened, "Pal, you're my best friend. I'm with Kitra. Whatever we work out, it includes you, whatever that means."

Flushing a deeper hue, Pinky said, "I want to believe that, but I am having trouble." The earlier oily overtones vanished, and his words became tentative. "Love is a human thing. At least, the love you're talking about. I only have my own definition. It is a matter of proximity. I sometimes feel that, if I push hard enough, I could become you, and you could become me." He paused. "I know that doesn't make sense."

"That *does* make sense," I said. I remembered the *Faucon*, and Pinky's physical and mental, maybe even spiritual union with L'Eclair. "I think we merge, too."

Out of the corner of my eye, I saw Fareedh waggle his eyebrows. I felt my face heating up. "Not like that. I mean, love is when part of you becomes part of the other person."

Peter snarked, "Yeah, Fareedh didn't used to make *nearly* as many fart jokes."

I looked sharply at Peter. Could no one take this seriously?! I looked back at Pinky, worried that the jokes would make him retreat again. Instead, I was surprised to find him pulsing happily. "It's true," Pinky said. "I guess he does have a bit of me in him."

"So, I think I'm getting the idea," Peter went on, looking at Pinky. "You're not talking about making out. You want us to love you and not leave you in the dust. To bring you in as part of this 'us' thing we're creating."

"Yes, I thought I had made that clear," Pinky sounded a little confused. He paused. Then, "I want to be in the circle with you."

Peter blew out a breath and spread his hands. "Well, Infinity. I'm fine with *that*. We're all people here. After everything, I'd be sad if you weren't in the circle." He grinned. "I love you, too."

There was a hush. Pinky said, "In other words, you're saying..." then faltered.

Marta took one of his oversized, three fingered hands in hers. "All

Pinkys are included." Then she added, "If they want to be."

He was flushing deep rose now, but his eyespots slid back to face me. "I don't go anywhere without Kitra. If I'm not the stumbling block, then it's up to her."

For some reason, the words made my stomach flip, and my throat was suddenly dry, realizing I'd put on a much braver front than I could maintain, now that the only decision left was mine. I couldn't even look up at them and risk seeing their anxious faces, risk letting them see the uncertainty in mine. I felt a wave of vertigo, like I was hanging by my toes at the edge of a great chasm. I'd thought I had it all figured out, but now that it was now-or-never, I wasn't sure of anything.

I coughed, swallowed, and managed, "Guys, I know I called this meeting, but I think I'm going to need a bit to gather my own thoughts."

And then I did flee, through the wardroom and back to my cabin.

I lay on my bed, staring up at the glowing ceiling and feeling every centimeter the fool. These were my best friends. I loved all of them. More than that, I knew I was in love with Marta, and the idea of being in love with the others…that wasn't unpleasant either. Fareedh was beautiful and loving. Peter was a great guy. And there was no one closer to me than Pinky. Why was I having so much trouble with this?

But I couldn't just jump into a five-way relationship. That'd be loony! I couldn't even handle a two-way relationship. I'd bungled things with Marta the first time, and this second time around, it felt like she was doing all the work. Now, they *all* had feelings for me? How was I supposed to respond? If they liked me more than I liked them, then I was sure to hurt feelings. They'd get upset. And then I'd lose them.

I closed my eyes, rubbing them with circling fingertips. That was it, of course. I was scared of losing them. Any of them. All of them. At first, I'd been afraid of getting involved with the others for fear of losing the special thing I had with Marta. Now the stakes were even higher. If I messed up trying to navigate a relationship — a real romantic relationship — with all of them, I'd be sure to alienate someone, and then everything would fall apart.

I shivered. I couldn't take losing anyone. I had to call it off. I had to pick up my *sayar* right now and…

I needed to calm down.

Sure, they'd started this, but I had expressed willingness to consider the possibility of an 'us' including the five of us, gathered them all together specifically to consider *this*. I couldn't just let panic dictate my decision. Even if it was awfully tempting.

I rolled over and buried my face in the pillow. My mind tugged at it for a long time, I don't know how long, replaying scenes, running through imaginary dialogues, oscillating between ideal and disastrous scenarios. Nothing seemed to resolve.

Somewhere along the way, I drifted off to sleep.

It was one of those situations where I knew I was dreaming, but only vaguely. The setting was familiar. We were all in Marta's little guest house, the one that had been her sister's before she moved to the other coast. Well, it was supposed to be that house, but in the manner of dreams, it was actually a giant treehouse, the main room nestled in a brace of branches.

We were playing some kind of game, seated on the floor with our knees touching. Only Pinky wasn't sitting; he was pacing a circle around us, tapping each of us on the shoulder as he passed. Then he placed a hand apiece on Peter and Fareedh's head, and in response, they leaned in to kiss. Marta giggled and blushed. I felt myself licking my lips, and my face grew hot.

When they were done, I felt Pinky's fingers on my head, and Marta looked at me expectantly. Without hesitation, I pulled her in. It was amazing and quickly got pretty steamy. At one point, I realized I wasn't wearing anything at all, though I was sure I had been when we'd started. I wasn't embarrassed, even with everyone right there. The boys pressed against us, and without breaking the kiss with Marta, my fingers began running through Peter's hair. It was a little longer than it had been, and very fine.

For some reason, adding him to the mix made everything five times as hot. I found my lips leaving Marta's, and I searched out Peter, the palm of my hand against his skull, pressing him toward me. I closed my eyes. Then just as his mouth found mine, my eyelids fluttered open…

I was staring at the ship's hull, just six inches from my face, fully conscious. I felt warm and tingly all over — especially so in certain areas. I blinked, then with a blush and a smile, I rolled on my back, the ceiling panels still glowing softly. My first thought: had I really been making out with *Peter*? I giggled. No, it wasn't so strange anymore.

In the dream — and in recent reality, I realized — Peter hadn't had any of that touchy defensiveness, that prickliness that had kept us from getting close. He was so sweet and gentle, especially given his size and strength. And handsome. Lord, how had I not noticed? His baby fat was gone, and he had that new beard, though it wasn't much past the scraggle phase.

I closed my eyes and deliberately imagined myself not just with Marta, but with Marta *and* Peter, wrapped in their arms and losing myself in their kisses. The thought didn't repel me. Quite the opposite. It felt natural now. My teeth caught at my lower lip, and my fingers started to slide together. Not with stress, but excitement.

Experimentally, I imagined Fareedh. That was even easier. The months before we'd first sailed on *Majera*, he'd been a frequent star of dreams, waking and otherwise. I just sort of pulled them out of storage and added them to the mix, and I could hear my breath blowing hot and hard through my nostrils.

In my mind's eye, Pinky's silly head suddenly popped out from behind them, and I couldn't tell if I'd deliberately brought him into the daydream, or if he'd somehow wormed his way in all by himself. I laughed out loud. Of course he would be there.

My fantasy went on, but changed in tone. Now we weren't making out, but just hugging, laughing, loving being together. The gang, but one unit, with no reservations. My smile broadened, and I felt tears coming. It was beautiful, and I realized my subconscious had known what I'd wanted all along.

Now, I couldn't imagine any other way of being than the way it was going to be, the way it already was: the five of us, partners. Nothing was going to break that, not even my cluelessness — not after all we'd been through, all that we were to each other. And if any of us struggled, well, we'd all be there to help each other through it, like we always had. I wasn't alone. None of us had to be alone anymore.

Shaking my head, grinning goofily, I rolled over onto my side and propped myself up on an elbow. I reached for my *sayar*, called up a group comm, and began composing my answer.

Epilogue

Third of Queen, 307 Post Settlement of Vatan (2847, old calendar)

It was hot and sticky in the narrow confines of my glider, even at 21:00, only a few hours after sunrise. The air came through the vent pipe like a desert wind. Still, I was happy for any ventilation. In fact, I was happy just to have my glider back, out of hock with hardly a comment from Sofia and Francois at the trade-in. It was like they'd expected me to come back for it.

We'd returned just in time. The winds were due to pick up in the next week, and they could be treacherously unpredictable. But right now, things were as smooth as the polar ice sheet, the early morning thermals gentle and unchallenging. The Sun glowed mutedly in the windscreen behind a dark disk of polarization, keeping the glare out of my eyes. From horizon to horizon stretched a dazzlingly clear green sky, finally the right color after so many weeks.

I craned my neck to look below and to my left out the window. The unworked fields south of Denizli were baked brown in the late summer, and the Goldayi trail snaked along toward the rougher, preserved land beyond. The sight sparked a sudden memory, of that fateful time the four of us — we hadn't met Fareedh yet — had hiked that trail during the break after graduation. The one Peter later thanked me for taking him on, though he certainly hadn't been grateful at the time. We'd all been awoken by a blood-curdling cry, too rough and reverberant to be human. Marta had been sure it was a puma, but as a native, I knew we didn't have any on Vatan. That didn't stop us from sharing the same tent for the rest of the night, Pinky stealing glances out the flap with an eyespot stalk as small as he could manage. We went home the next day, never learning what it had been.

Home. It was hard to believe we were home after everything. I could almost imagine that we'd never left, that everything was back to how it had been. It was even the Queen holidays, like right when we'd left a year ago. But when I tried, all of the events of the last year pressed in at the edges, one after another bursting into the forefront of my mind. A kaleidoscope of images and attendant responsibilities: the colony on Sirena, the new fleet parked over Hyvilma, the Pesad-umbrans enduring the pebbly gale in their makeshift exile, waiting to be rescued.

One year — it sounded like both a long time and the blink of an eye. One year ago to the day, I sat with Fareedh in the half-finished bridge of our new ship and came up with the name, *Majera*: Turkish for 'adventure'.

I tugged the yoke and pressed a rudder pedal, and my glider responded agilely. Now the glittering line of the ocean was ahead. On my left, kilometers away, was Denizli, where I'd been aerotowed into the sky from, an hour before. It was ironic that, after all that agonizing over *Majera's* name, I had never come up with one for my glider. Because its number is SV-CLROC, Pinky sometimes called it The Roc, which suited me fine. A Roc was a bird, after all.

With the plane now on its new course, I settled back into a daydream. Well, not so much a daydream, but a *pondering*. Somehow, it was easier to make big life decisions from a pilot's seat. Maybe it was being removed from everything, or maybe it was having complete control over a tiny portion of my universe.

And I had a doozy of a decision to make. Again.

The last several weeks had been kind of loony. We'd come back to find we were hometown heroes for what had happened on *Hyvilma*. Madame Mayor must have had plans on a hair trigger, because within a half day of telling Vatan spaceport that we were landing, we'd been invited to a parade downtown, scheduled three days hence.

So, there we were, just getting used to double-long Vatan days, escorted by a platoon of local Legionnaires in their purple finery, waving like royalty to a crowd that must have been in the thousands. I have to say, there's no better cure for space lag than public adoration. We rode that high for a week, which was good because that was the busiest week I'd ever spent planetside. Everyone wanted to talk to us. The High Commissioner wanted a report about the Pesadumbrans for the Governor on Sennet, and ultimately higher than that. The Commissioner promised that their department would act quickly, and that they had the best interests of the aliens at heart. Marta, whether out of her normal skepticism for the government, or because of her being the one trained biologist who'd actually met the Pesadumbrans, insisted on staying in the loop. What that meant, exactly, we wouldn't know for weeks. Hopefully not seasons.

Meanwhile, the Deputy for Eastern Vatan was most interested in our experience on the *Faucon*. He made a casual suggestion that some of us might want to run for local Delegate next year — with his party, of course. We said we'd think about it. Then we laughed on the way home from the meeting; I was the only one with anything like governmental aspirations, and none of us were cut out for ground-side politics.

We retained a lawyer; Peter's Super Jump discovery was too valuable to just give away. Even keeping mum about that, Peter still had plenty of research to turn in to his professors in lieu of university coursework — the whole reason he'd come with us in the first place! He made a good paper out of the data he'd gotten from the crack in space where the Émilie's Jump drive had been. Marta turned in a draft report on Jub-Jub and the ecosystem on Isabella. Both of them got a year's credit for their work, which kept them on track for graduation next year.

Now Fareedh was out home-hunting. Pooling our housing allowance, and adding in the stipend I got as a Reserve Naval Lieutenant — learning I was entitled to that was a nice surprise — we could actually afford something decent. And it would be all our own. It was kind of funny. Before *Majera*, we'd occasionally talked about moving out of our homes, especially me with my chafing with Uncle Yusuf. We'd even thrown the idea around of getting a cheap place together. But we certainly hadn't dreamed it would be with all of us in a relationship.

In love, I amended. I smiled at that, and then felt goosebumps prickle the hair all along my arms, remembering our night together before our last Egress. I shivered, joggling the plane a little bit.

I trimmed the ailerons, keeping the ship on a stable course, checked the altimeter, and went back on autopilot.

I was glad to have the government taking things off my hands, thrilled as anything at the idea of coming home to Marta and Peter and Fareedh and Pinky. It would be like living on *Majera*, only with more room. *Starships and Supernovas* or *Empires* every day! I had even been thinking of writing a book, maybe inspired by our trips. The idea of being a real author, like the people who wrote the interstellar romances I read, was amazing. All of that was great.

But…

Yesterday, I'd gotten a spacegramme, all the way from Sennet by priority mail boat.

The memory of a face, fleshy and bearded, full of animation, swam back into my mind's eye. It was accompanied by a big, hearty voice that was used to talking, that shot words out faster than a gatling laser, that bowled you over from their sheer force and number.

The face and voice belonged to André Piedrouge, writer and senior partner at Naxa Productions, and he spent the first half of the twenty minute 'gramme praising a person I'd scarcely recognized as me: A duralloy-spined hero. A natural xenoethnologist, the first person to discover an alien race in decades. The galaxy's sharpest planet-finder. The savior of the Empire, who had shut down a civil war single-handed.

After ten minutes of that, my cheeks had felt like they were glowing with heat. It had not occurred to me that our exploits would make us — well, me at least — so famous. I probably should have expected it. To hear Piedrouge tell it, I was Ansari, Marquant, and Angelina IV all rolled into one.

He almost made me *believe* it.

Then he told me who *he* was. He rattled off a series of names, the people he worked with. They were only vaguely familiar, but then again, I don't follow pop culture much. But then he mentioned the holos he'd produced and co-written, and I did a double-take. *Everyone's* familiar with *The Name of the Witch* and *Lovely Molly's Fear*, the two books in the Genesis Killer series. That second one had left on a cliff-hanger, and we'd been waiting for five years for the third, which promised to be the best.

That's when he made his pitch. He wanted to drop everything

and become my personal agent. All of his other projects were second-rate compared to my story, he said. With the snap of his fingers, he could schedule a dozen-planet junket, all expenses paid by Naxa, that would transform me from a local sensation to a galactic star. Interviews, tours, recorded shows, live shows, the works.

And that would just be the beginning. Anything I wanted — fame, fortune, maybe even an honorary title — awaited. The Empire was mine on a platter.

Piedrouge knew all the buttons to push. He'd even seemed to read my mind, telling me that fame would help me sell books, if I wanted to write them. And the thought of being a noble, letting me rub elbows with the big wheels, as mom used to…wow. Finally, he'd teased, all this would pave the way to more and better *Majera* flights, which he would be happy to facilitate.

All I needed to do was respond with a 'yes', and he'd take care of the rest.

Swept away in the moment, tongue dry from my mouth hanging open for so long, I almost, *almost*, dashed off a "yes" right away.

Then I came to my senses. My friends and I had *just* decided to start a new chapter together. I dreaded the idea of another big decision, Yet Another Talk, threatening the status quo before it'd really begun. I had serious doubts that they'd even want to come. I was lucky to have gotten Peter as long as I had, and all of them had plans that didn't involve going off Vatan for a good long while.

Beyond that, Piedrouge hadn't invited the gang. He'd invited *me*. To be fair, the news coverage had downplayed the others' involvement in our adventures, particularly the Hyvilma incident. It made political sense, and Captain Sirocco had told me to expect it, but it still rankled a little. Maybe I could convince Piedrouge to take on the whole team. Maybe not. In any event, it was one more thing to worry about.

It'd kept me up half the night. What was I going to do?

I shook my head, a violent little motion that brushed my loose hair against my ears and shoulders. I didn't have to *do* anything, at least for now. There was no clock I was racing against. Food wasn't running low. People weren't going to die.

Plus, *I* didn't have to make the decision. *We* would make the decision, like we always did. And it would be fine, like it always was.

André the Agent could wait a few more weeks. I was going to enjoy a nice vacation, revel in the company of my friends, soak in the wonder of my new relationship. I'd earned that. For once in my life, I felt I'd done enough.

The future would still be there when I was ready for it.

I came back to reality, focusing my eyes on the horizon straight ahead, the sunshine turning the interface of the ocean and sky into a line of flame, like the end of the universe. I stared until my eyes watered. Then I blinked, leaned forward, and banked The Roc into a graceful, leftward arc.

I was going home.

Jub-Jub!

About the Series

Back when my father was a kid, they had science fiction books for young adults and kids. They called them "juveniles", and they usually featured a young hero flying to the stars. I grew up on these and loved them.

Over the years, YA became all about dystopia and fantasy. I enjoyed The Hunger Games and Harry Potter as much as everyone else, but I missed the space adventures. I wanted to see stories that weren't zero-sum game fights against a Big Bad, that featured reasonably accurate science and characters who struggled with realistic problems. Tales of friendship, ingenuity, and wonder.

Kitra was my first book. It was more successful than I could have dreamed. Years after it came out, it's still getting glowing reviews. It resonates with people. The found family, the diversity in representation, the "strange new worlds," Pinky's jokes: all of these made readers happy again and again.

But there was one common refrain: people wanted to know more. About Kitra and her ragtag crew. The nature of Pinky. The planets beyond the Frontier.

And so I wrote *Sirena*, *Hyvilma*, and now *Majera*. I hope you enjoy it as much as I enjoyed creating it!

~

The lifeblood of every author is audience feedback. Please consider leaving a review (of whatever length) on Amazon, GoodReads, or your favorite platform.

About the Publisher

Founded in 2019 by Galactic Journey's Gideon Marcus, **Journey Press** publishes the best science fiction, current and classic, with an emphasis on the unusual and the diverse.

Also available from Journey Press:

***Kitra* by Gideon Marcus - A YA Space Adventure**

Stranded in space: no fuel, no way home…and no one coming to help!

Nineteen-year-old Kitra Yilmaz dreams of traveling the galaxy like her Ambassador mother. But soaring in her glider is the closest she can get to touching the stars — until she stakes her inheritance on a salvage Navy spaceship.

***Sirena* by Gideon Marcus - Book 2 in the Kitra Saga**

One starship, six friends, 10,000 lives in the balance.

Young captain-for-hire Kitra Yilmaz has gotten her first contract: escort the mysterious Princess of Atlántida beyond the Frontier and find her a new world. It's a risky job, fraught with the threat of pirates, dangerous squatters, and rising romantic tensions.

***Hyvilma* by Gideon Marcus - Book 3 in the Kitra Saga**

A damaged ship, a dying shipmate–can she save both?

The flight back to Hyvilma should have been the easy part for the crew of the Majera — until a deadly ambush by pirates sends them reeling through hyperspace. Now getting to the planet in time is the only way Captain Kitra Yilmaz can save her dying friend.

BABEL-17
SAMUEL R. DELANY
Think galactic—or your world is lost!
MARVEL COMICS GROUP
FOU
12¢
Introducing THE SENSATIONAL BLACK PANTHER!
THE MAGAZINE
ntasy AN
ence Fictio
50¢
DO YOU WANT TO TRAVEL BACK IN TIME?
WWW.GALACTICJOURNEY.ORG

www.ingramcontent.com/pod-product-compliance
Lightning Source LLC
Chambersburg PA
CBHW021150190726
48288CB00008B/2909